D1576095

DISCARD

LOVE
&
HAIGHT

LOVE & HAIGHT

Susan Carlton

Henry Holt and Company ∞ New York

Ingram 6/12/13 9/699

YA
Fic
Carlton

Henry Holt and Company, LLC
Publishers since 1866
175 Fifth Avenue
New York, New York 10010
macteenbooks.com

Henry Holt® is a registered trademark of Henry Holt and Company, LLC.

Copyright © 2012 by Susan R. F. K. Carlton
All rights reserved.

Library of Congress Cataloging-in-Publication Data
Carlton, Susan R. F. K.
Love and Haight / Susan Carlton. — 1st ed.
p.   cm.
Summary: Seventeen-year-old Chloe brings her friend MJ to San Francisco, one of the
few places where an abortion can be obtained legally in 1971, to get rid of Chloe's
"Thing" while staying with her bohemian Aunt Kiki, experiencing hippie culture,
and reconnecting with a former boyfriend.
ISBN 978-0-8050-8097-1 (hc)
[1. Abortion—Fiction. 2. Pregnancy—Fiction. 3. Hippies—Fiction. 4. Aunts—
Fiction. 5. San Francisco (Calif.)—History—20th century—Fiction.] I. Title.
PZ7.C216853Lov 2012   [Fic]—dc23   2011025595

First Edition—2012 / Designed by Véronique Lefèvre Sweet

Printed in the United States of America

10 9 8 7 6 5 4 3 2 1

4858804

I'd rather be a lightning rod than a seismograph.

—Ken Kesey

For my mother, an original Ms.

LOVE & HAIGHT

OPPOSABLE THUMBS

The view was wrong. That's what Chloe kept thinking. Where was the phantasmagoric bridge? Where was the Rice-A-Roni cable car?

She'd been waiting eleven hours for this moment. Eleven hours in the Lady Bug from Phoenix, bending north past Hollywood, then Santa Barbara, then Santa Cruz, then, finally, San Francisco. Eleven hours of loading up on Tab and pulling over to pee. Eleven hours of speculating about what trouble two girls could stir up on their pre–New Year's road trip. Every twenty minutes, MJ would come up with a cheer, a leftover habit from her majorette days. The punch line was always 1972. I'm gonna wanna screw . . . in 1972. We'll party, woo-hoo-hoo . . . in 1972. Let's all have cheese fondue . . . in 1972.

And then . . .

"*There* it is!" Chloe said, getting a far-off glimpse of the Golden Gate Bridge busting into the sky.

MJ started the count. "And a five, six, seven, eight."

In unison they unlocked their respective sides of the Bug's

convertible roof. MJ climbed into the back seat, yanking the canvas roof along with her, and snapped it into place.

The air was minty fresh from all the eucalyptus trees at the side of the road. Chloe breathed in deeply.

"No turning back now!" MJ took a fistful of Cracker Jack, of happy food, and threw it like confetti.

"Cut it out." Chloe batted away the sticky bits.

The bridge slipped from view, but there was no doubt they were hurtling ahead, top down, to spend Christmas break in the most grooved-out city on the planet.

MJ fiddled with the radio. Static/classical music, static/jingle bells, static/traffic report, static/sitar. Finally, she hit an FM station at the top of the dial and the Who came through. *I said, now I've got my MAGIC Bus. . . .*

The road thrummed under the wheels.

"It's so huge!" MJ said, when the bridge emerged again.

"It's not even golden," Chloe said. "It's *orange*. A color called International Orange, not golden at all. That's what it said in the Triple-A guide."

The freeway zigzagged right, left, right, right, left, then straight to the bridge.

They'd gone twenty miles out of their way, looping north to go south just to enter the city via the bridge—but instead of gunning the engine, Chloe flicked on her turn signal.

"What are you doing?" MJ yelled over the Who. The Saint Christopher medal she'd hung from the rearview mirror swung to and fro.

"Pulling over."

MJ shot her a quick look. "Uh, we're halfway on a bridge."

"No, we're either on a bridge or we're not. And we're not."

So far, senior year was all either / or. Either a fox or a prude. Either a partier or a dud. Either a hippie or a conformist. Either on the magic bus or off it.

Chloe downshifted—fourth, then third, then second and stopped in the makeshift emergency shoulder just before the on-ramp.

"Holy shit! You're crazy," MJ said, getting out the passenger door.

Chloe climbed over the gearshift and got out on the guardrail side, too. A pickup truck zoomed by, and the ground quivered.

The air, the realness, made her queasy. Chloe took the sunglasses from the top of her head and slid them over her eyes.

"I'm okay," MJ said. "Are you okay?"

They'd had to read the crappy self-help book *I'm OK—You're OK* in Girls' Health. It had become their inside joke. At a party one or the other of them would say, "I've had four beers. I'm okay . . . are you okay?"

"I want to be," Chloe said. "I want to, you know, woo-hoo-hoo in 1972."

"We'll find plenty of time to woo-hoo. We're staying with Kiki, remember?" MJ fingered the little peace sign she always wore, twisting it around and around. "You want me to drive?"

"No." A shot of orange flew by Chloe's eye and she turned to see a blur of butterfly. "I don't want to get back in the car."

MJ raised an eyebrow.

Cars motored on—a pair of Mustangs, a station wagon with wood paneling, a souped-up something painted red—but no one stopped to ask if they needed help.

Chloe's Snoopy watch said three fifty. She was supposed to call Kiki at four.

MJ sat on the hood and cracked her knuckles. "Here's the deal I just made up," she announced.

"Yeah?"

"One, two, three, four, I declare a thumb war. If I win, you get in the car, and I'll drive."

Sitting there on the hood, they waged five thumb wars. She and MJ had been battling since first grade. They were the queens of opposable thumbs.

Chloe let MJ win. Actually, MJ always won.

After a logging truck nearly sideswiped them, logs jostling for freedom from the chains, Chloe stood up."

MJ climbed in first, over the gearshift, to the driver's seat. She slid the seat back to make room for her basketball legs and readjusted the mirror. Before they took off, MJ unlooped the Saint Christopher and pressed it into Chloe's hand.

"He's the patron saint of long journeys," MJ said.

"Not for me," Chloe said, dropping the pendant in the ash-free ashtray.

"Well, it can't hurt."

MJ gunned it, and they were back on track. The bridge's cables loomed like double-Dutch jump ropes. Chloe had to pace herself, decide when to jump in. "I haven't told anyone else," she said. "Did I tell you that?"

MJ nodded. "Except Shep, the original dipstick."

"Not Kiki. And not Virginia either." Since the divorce, her mother had wanted to be called Virginia. In her head Chloe added, *And defi-nitely not Teddy.*

MJ's answer was to turn the radio up, loud. Elton John filled the silence. They loved this song—*Hold me closer tiny dancer, count the headlights on the hiiiiighway*—and they sang along.

As they waited in line to pay the toll, Chloe thought that driving across the Golden Gate was a little like sex. It was supposed to be this major mind-blowing experience but then it was over in three minutes, and it didn't really measure up to the hype.

On the other side of the bridge, MJ pulled over by the marina. Chloe fed the pay phone a dime and called Kiki. After ten rings, there was officially no answer.

She and MJ split a falafel from a little place on Chestnut Street.

Chloe called again. Then again.

They split another falafel, this one deluxe.

"I guess she's out," Chloe said. She remembered her aunt's old apartment was near strip clubs and fresh linguini, but Kiki had moved twice since then.

"We've got time to kill," MJ said. She flipped her head over and shook her hair, giving it more oomph. "How about a cocktail?"

Three blocks up, they passed a place called the Riff.

"Wait," Chloe said before they stepped inside. "What if we get carded?"

MJ wheeled around. "We'll figure it out."

Chloe had never been to a bar before, not even in Tempe, where the university frat boys partied.

Inside, Hendrix's "Wild Thing" thumped through the speakers. It took a minute for her eyes to adjust. Walls, ceiling, counter . . . all orange. Even the lighting was an intense orange, like a delicious carrot.

Chloe pulled up a bar stool by the door in case she needed a quick escape from the wild things.

"Every single person here has long hair," Chloe said, swiveling around. Wavy or straight or parted in the middle, plus one guy with strands of sourgrass woven through his braids.

"Good—we belong," MJ said, flinging her hair around.

A college-age guy with a fringed jacket and banged-up cowboy boots sidled up.

"Hey, want to sign my petition?" he asked them, flicking his thumb and forefinger like a gun. It was a crappy line, but the guy was kind of a fox. His hair was wavy and it whooshed over his forehead like Jim Morrison before the OD.

MJ gave Chloe an exaggerated wink, as if to say, *See? No reason to freak.* She yelled over the bass, "Buy us a margarita, and now you're talking."

"I like your spirit," he said to MJ.

"I like your boots," MJ said back.

"I like your shininess." The guy plucked a strap of MJ's silver halter. She didn't flinch.

Chloe tried the pay phone again.

A pair of margaritas arrived in speckled glasses. Chloe let hers sit there.

MJ leaned into the guy. "We're . . . we're, uh, twins. I'm Belinda, and this is Tralinda."

"Tra*linda*?" Chloe repeated.

"Tralinda is uptight," MJ said. She took the straw from her drink and traced *t-i-g-h-t* on the bar. "So, who are you?"

The guy tucked his hand into MJ's back pocket. "Me, I'm the guy your mother warned you about."

"Heard that before," she said. MJ was doing what she always did—flirting with any passing penis.

Chloe tried to find her groove, to lose the negative energy, as Virginia would say. She wound her hair into a loose bun, jabbing a cocktail spear into the center, trying to hold it all in place.

"Like your hair," boot man said to her.

"I'm cutting it," Chloe said. Pieces of hair fell to the front, and Chloe fingered the waves. She took an itty-bitty sip of the cocktail. It was vinegary.

MJ's glass was empty. "Whoa-no-no. Clo—uh, Melinda's—hair is her thing. She wouldn't get rid of it."

"I *would*," Chloe said.

"I thought she was Tralinda, but it's cool either way," boot man said. "Another round?"

Chloe excused herself to call again. She came back to the bar with a shrug.

"I wish my brother was still in Berkeley," MJ said to no one in particular, sucking down the dregs of Chloe's drink. "We could crash with him."

"Too bad," Chloe said. The fact that Teddy was spending the holidays in Sacramento with his roommate was one small piece of the week that was going Chloe's way.

"I'll put you up," boot guy said with a smile. "Or there's a hostel around the corner on Eddy Street."

"Actually, we have to go." Chloe stood and jiggled her jeans into place. "We've got a big day tomorrow."

MJ slammed the bar and her glass shuddered. "*Some* of us do. *Some* of us have big things to do."

"C'mon," Chloe said. "Let's split."

MJ hitchhiked her thumb to Chloe. "This one, she's getting the Big A."

"Acid?" boot man asked. "Oooh, I love the bad girls."

"No!" MJ swatted at his knee. "Sometimes the good girls are the bad girls and the bad girls . . . Ah, shit, I don't know what I mean. Tralinda, the good girl here, she's getting the hanger."

"The what?"

"Sshhh!" MJ held her middle finger to her lips so she was simultaneously shushing and flipping the bird.

"Shut up!" Chloe yanked MJ by the elbow. "She talks shit when she's drunk."

"Whoa," boot man said. "You girls are cute but . . . fuckin' strange. . . ." He turned his back on them, moving in the direction of a girl with sleeves as wide as wings.

Outside, Chloe said, "What the hell were you doing in there? And, just so you know, there is no hanger."

"I *know*," MJ said.

"If you have a problem with my getting unpregnant . . ." Chloe twisted her hair back into its bun, hard.

MJ held Chloe's shoulders, probably not as squarely as she wished. She was six inches taller than Chloe, and when she talked bits of spit landed on Chloe's eyelashes. "What do you want, Clo? I'm here on your emergency vacation. I'm here."

"Here, badmouthing me to Monsieur Cowboy Boots."

MJ hiccupped quietly. "The Catholic girl guilt is getting to me. Maybe it's the margaritas talking."

Chloe's stomach knotted up. She didn't want to hear MJ's judgment, even if it was tequila judgment. "We're tired. Let's find the damn hostel."

They drove to Eddy Street in edgy silence. Chloe wasn't even sure what they were looking for. A hotel? A dorm? Down a few blocks they saw a timber-brown building with a carved wooden sign out front.

The place looked normal enough on the outside, except for a guy using his dog as a pillow by the doorway. Inside, the walls were painted a pulsating blue. A kid with a beard sat in the lotus position on one of those cable-spool coffee tables.

"Greetings," he said, not getting up. He gestured toward a poster that listed rates and rules.

Chloe handed over seven dollars. She had a sudden craving for Bugles, the cone-shaped chips, wanting to slip one on each finger and bite them off like she was four years old.

Upstairs, there were three large mattresses on the floor and no people. Two of the beds seemed reserved with backpacks and paperbacks, possibly in German. MJ and Chloe put their duffels on the available mattress propped up on cinder blocks. The grubby Navajo blanket made Chloe wish she'd brought a sleeping bag.

MJ jumped on the bed and did a decent cartwheel.

Chloe sat on the edge of the bed. "We haven't even said the word."

"You want me to say it?" MJ asked. "Abortion, abortion, abortion."

"All right."

"Abortion, abortion, abortion." MJ paused. "Abor-shunnn," she sang with a flourish. She dropped next to Chloe on the bed.

"All right."

"Really? Because I don't even know what's going on tomorrow."

"Here's what I know," Chloe said. "I go to a clinic tomorrow. They give me the name of a doctor. I see that doctor. I see another doctor. And maybe another one, I'm not sure. And then, a week later, if nothing goes wrong, it's done."

MJ rolled her hands up in the bottom of her shirt, like it was a muff. "That's if everything goes right. That's if this is even the right thing."

"This is," Chloe said. She didn't mention that she'd taken to calling the lima, the lentil, the zygote, *This*. She liked that *This* suggested something but also nothing. *This* didn't grow or change. *This* didn't become that, it stayed *This*.

They sat there for a few minutes before MJ said, "You know why I'm a bitch? I'm *starving*."

"There's a vending machine in the lobby. Plain or peanut?"

"Definitely peanut."

In the lobby, a bunch of girls in gauzy skirts were ring-around-the-rosying, and it struck Chloe that not a single one of them was pregnant—probably not, anyway. She might be the unluckiest girl in a city filled with mythically beautiful, twirly girls. She got candy, then grabbed a makeshift ice bucket—a beer stein from a stack by the stairs. She pushed the bull's-eye button on the ice machine and watched the cubes slide down the chute.

The afternoon that began the *This*, Shep had dropped an ice cube down Chloe's shirt. She screamed and jumped around, trying to dance the cube out. He went looking for it, and she felt the ice sliding and Shep's hands sliding. And then he unlaced her lace-up shirt and they made out. And Neil Young was on. "Sugar Mountain"—a long song.

Ice in one hand, candy in the other, Chloe returned to find MJ jumping again. Chloe kicked off her clogs and joined in, trying to synchronize with MJ, but her rhythm was off. MJ's legs were longer, and she put that majorette thrust into each jump. The ice flew out of the beer stein and skipped over the bed.

"Give me the candy!" MJ said, not missing a beat. She opened the bag with her teeth and flipped a couple of M&M's in Chloe's direction.

Chloe missed once, then again and again, opening her mouth a beat after the candy hit the bed. All this jumping was making her stomach lurchy. She got off the bed and flipped on a little TV swinging from a macramé plant hanger, wanting to hear someone else's voice in the room. They watched a little *Bonanza*, then a year-end special on the best of Johnny Carson.

Mr. Late Night himself was in the middle of some skit, wearing a turban. "May a diseased yak befriend your sister," he said.

"To yaks!" MJ said, her ankles bobbling.

"*Ja!* To yaks!" the tall, presumably German, guys said from the doorway.

"To"—Chloe stopped. Her mouth filled with bile. She ran across the hall to the bathroom. The candy-coated M&M shells were still recognizable, bright fragments in the beige muck. She hugged the toilet, wishing for a minute that Virginia, or someone not really like Virginia, was there to hold her hair back.

DIALING FOR DOCTORS

It was almost seven in the morning, and Chloe felt like she'd slept all of two minutes. The cuter of the German boys, it turned out, snored like a hippo.

Climbing over a sprawled-out MJ, Chloe crossed to the bathroom for a morning heave. She threw up, then rocked back on her heels waiting for the next wave. Since the morning sickness had started last week, the nausea came in twos.

As Chloe backed out of the stall, the snoring German was suddenly right there. "I am Rolf. All is good with you now?"

At the sink, Chloe cupped her hands to scoop water, swished, and spit. "Sure."

"You are a very pretty girl with a not-pretty illness. I have hashish. It will be good for you." He pulled up his shirt and patted his pale stomach. "I will roll you something with hashish and tobacco, and it will be very nice for you. In a matter of fact, it will be excellent."

"Oh, no thanks," Chloe said, splashing her face with cold water. The last thing Chloe needed was a party-hearty stick.

"I want to give you something. Please, I will give this to you?" He offered up a striped washcloth. He was probably about to use it to wash his cute German face.

"No," she said with a shake of her head.

"It will be a gift."

What could she say? "Danke."

When Rolf left, Chloe dried her face with the cloth. It was clean and very soft, and she kept it in her left hand, running her finger along the edge. Without knowing why, Chloe shoved it into the pocket of her Levi's, like a slip of a security blanket.

Back in the room, MJ was up and dressed and looking improbably flirty in a crocheted jumper. "Let's find a Tab so I can unbitch." She flipped her hair around. "And speaking of bitches, sorry for being one last night."

"You don't have to come with me," Chloe said.

"Here we go, right? I want to meet the real doctor."

"Cool," Chloe said, even though she was seeing a social worker.

The girls walked into Far-Fetched Foods, but there was no Tab in sight—no Coke either, only carrot juice and unfiltered cider. MJ bought some trail mix, on the theory that at least it had chocolate chips.

On another day, Chloe might have asked MJ to drive because she was feeling quaky in the stomach. But *This* was her problem, her row to hoe, as Virginia would have said a few years ago, when she still said things that could be cross-stitched on little wall hangings. Besides,

MJ seemed hungover, staring a little too intently at each speck of trail mix before popping it in her mouth.

It wasn't until after Chloe tobogganed down the hills and slid on and off the cable car track and parallel parked in front of the building with her wheels cut to the curb that she realized she didn't have a good idea what to expect. For all her note taking about the situation in general, she was sketchy about the specifics for her specifically.

Even the office was a surprise, three attached Victorians all painted shades of mauve. She'd figured it would be more office looking. A discreet brass plaque out front listed the clinic hours as eight thirty until three—school hours, Chloe thought.

It was 8:17.

Chloe and MJ played three quick games of thumb war. MJ won, won, won.

Chloe and MJ had to be buzzed in, like at a fancy apartment building. The counseling office was on the second floor.

"Wouldn't it be wild if you weren't really pregnant?" MJ said on the stair landing.

"I am."

"You could be wrong."

"Not according to Dr. Gladstone."

When Chloe had first panicked that she might be pregnant, when her like-clockwork period was two days, then five days late, she'd called her pediatrician. Chloe figured she could trust Dr. Gladstone, who had once offered her the Pill out of Virginia's earshot. The doctor told Chloe to come by the office first thing the next morning before eating or drinking for a pee-in-a-cup test.

The test took a few hours to develop, Dr. Gladstone said. Chloe went to school, then back to the doctor's little yellow house at the end of the day.

He sat her down in the empty waiting room. "Positive."

Chloe had figured as much, since her boobs had been throbbing for a week. She'd spent her last few study halls in the library reading through *Time* and the *New York Times* in the Current Events corner and had two pages of notes about abortion.

"Are you thinking of going forward with the pregnancy?" Dr. Gladstone asked.

Could she go backward? She shook her head.

"If you want to do an adoption, I have the name of a lawyer," Dr. Gladstone said. "If you think you might want to terminate—"

"I do." Chloe's face was hot.

Virginia had been talking about abortion for a while, about the theoretical right of it, but last summer she and her women's group bounced their braless boobs all day collecting "signatures of solidarity" for a Jane Roe who was suing the state of Texas over something to do with abortions.

But taking a public stand was different from having a family talk. When Chloe was in fifth grade, she asked Virginia if it was true you could get pregnant from French kissing (possibly, according to MJ's sister), and Virginia answered, "Wait one second. . . . I have something for you."

Chloe dug her toes into the shag carpet on the stairs, anticipating the Talk, until Virginia reappeared with her copy of the Kama Sutra.

"Meet the Bible," Virginia said, holding the slim volume to her chest.

"I wish my mother had let me in on its secrets." Virginia was big on leading by osmosis.

The Kama Sutra, Chloe discovered, was a Sanskrit guide to karma and dharma with some sex stuff in the middle. There were drawings of people getting it on in various positions—Pair-of-Tongs, Splitting-a-Bamboo—and descriptions of the man placing his lingam into a woman's yoni. In the illustrations the people had tons—really, *tons*—of pubic hair, and it creeped Chloe out.

Dr. Gladstone said, "Well, then it's either Mexico or California. I wish you had more options, but there you have it. Of the two, I strongly suggest California. I can give you a name if it would be helpful."

"Thanks," Chloe said, writing down the number of the Women's Way.

"Will you talk to Virginia, or shall I?" he asked.

"I'll handle it," Chloe said, which wasn't officially a lie. She would handle it, just without Virginia.

The waiting room was empty. A young woman sat coiled on a swivel chair behind a desk, ready to spring.

"I have an appointment," Chloe said, imagining how Virginia would handle this, trying to capture the confident tone her mother had perfected in her assertiveness-training workshops. "Chloe Switzer," she added.

"We'll be with you in a moment," the receptionist said.

"Uh, there's no one here," MJ said, looking around at the rows of empty chairs.

The buzzer sounded, and a pair of women, a mother-type and a lookalike daughter, appeared a moment later. They both wore shorts, thick wool socks, and boots, like they were on their way to a hike.

"I have an eight forty-five," the younger woman told the receptionist. "Pill refill." The receptionist waved them to a hallway on the left, and Chloe found herself fantasizing about life with a mom who would be willing to take the back seat, feministically speaking.

"Okay," the receptionist said to Chloe. "Ready for you." She helixed up and Chloe and MJ followed her down the hall to a small cubicle.

There, a petite girl with a ballet bun and glasses twirled around to introduce herself as Annie-Fraser-but-call-me-Annie. "Welcome. How did you find us?"

"My doctor in Phoenix," Chloe said. She decided against saying *pediatrician*. "I'm pregnant, and I would like an . . . I would like to be unpregnant."

MJ sneezed.

"Bless you." Annie opened a fresh manila folder and spread it across her small lap. Chloe noticed that she had neat handwriting—"new patient" was written all in lowercase—and she felt a kinship. "And you are?"

"Chloe. Rhymes with David Bowie and is spelled *C-h-l-o-e*." She was used to hearing her name pronounced *Chow-ly* or *Chlow*.

"I know, like the French fashion house," Annie said. "So, how pregnant are you?"

"Three and three-quarter weeks."

Annie crinkled her nose. "But *when* was your last period?" As a visual aid, Annie un-thumb-tacked a calendar with black-and-white photographs of ballerina feet from a bulletin board and handed it over.

Chloe traced her finger along the boxes. "This one. The Saturday before Thanksgiving."

"So . . . November twentieth," Annie said. "That makes you five and a half weeks, going on six."

"I know you've just met Chloe, but she can be trusted when it comes to math," MJ offered.

Chloe liked that: being trusted.

Annie had a sweet smile. "I'm sure you're both right, but gestational age is counted from LMP—last menstrual period. Always," she added, unnecessarily.

Chloe's hands flapped. "No, I couldn't have been pregnant that long. It was December fourth."

"It's still very early, well within the range we can work with. Let me go over a few things."

"I lost two weeks." Chloe lifted her felt-tip, poised to take good notes out of habit, but she felt defeated.

At the side table, MJ had picked up a model of a uterus the size of a grapefruit and was turning it over and over.

"First, you are not alone." Annie patted Chloe's hand. She wore many thin silver rings. "Last year there were a hundred thousand abortions in San Francisco."

"A hundred thousand?" MJ flipped the uterus around. "A hundred *thousand*. Think about that, Clo. That's, like, all of Phoenix."

Chloe slipped her hand out from Annie's clasp. She wanted her hands to herself.

Annie readjusted herself and crossed her legs. "So let's get right to it. The doctor I'm referring you to does the procedure in what we call the come-and-go part of the hospital. You'll *come*, then you'll *go* in a few hours. His fee is two hundred fifty dollars." Annie caught Chloe's eye. "That's on the low side."

Chloe had sixty dollars more than she needed, a hundred of it from Shep. When Chloe had told him what she was doing over Christmas vacation, he'd said, "Shit, shit, shit." The next day, he handed her an envelope stuffed with tens.

"What about the shrink?" Chloe asked.

"Ah, you've done your homework." Annie struck Chloe as someone who had always done her homework. "That's the loophole. . . . Well, I won't say loophole."

"Uh, you just did," MJ pointed out.

"That's the *detail* that makes abortion legal here. You need to find a reason the pregnancy is a risk to you. And since you seem healthy—"

"I am." Chloe wanted Annie to like her.

"Then, yes, a psychiatrist can help you establish that the pregnancy is a risk to your health. To your sanity."

"Whoa!" MJ dropped the uterus on the linoleum and scooped it back up. "You're not insane, you're pregnant! And now a doctor has to diagnose you as crazy?" Chloe couldn't tell if her tone was dubious or disgusted.

"It's a formality, right?" Chloe asked. Dr. Gladstone had made it sound like no big deal.

Annie nodded. "We're lucky to be in a city with many mental health professionals—you have your pick. Since you're well prepared . . ."

Chloe beamed, her teacher's-pet feathers in fine form.

"I'm sure your doctor mentioned parental involvement." Annie swooped her hand through the air.

Chloe was conscious of breathing evenly. "Sort of. Not really."

"You don't have a tape recorder tucked into that uterus, do you?" Annie asked MJ with a laugh. "Because this is absolutely off the record, and the rules change every other month. But as of right now, the hospital needs to see that you've got a parent with you."

MJ kicked Chloe under the chair.

Chloe flipped through the lined pages of her notebook. "I heard girls come here on their own. Where did I read that? I think it was *Seventeen*. No, probably not." *Seventeen*, she'd discovered in her research, was edited by an ex-nun. "Maybe it was the *New York Times*."

"I haven't finished—" Annie interrupted.

"Or *Time*," Chloe said.

"If you don't have a parent willing or able, you can bring what's called a Parental Notification Document. An official note, witnessed by someone over age eighteen, that grants a child—well, you—permission to abort."

Chloe slowly nodded. Both she and MJ were pretty good at forging class excuses. *Please excuse my daughter from gym, as it is, once again, that time of the month.* Mrs. O'Haig didn't catch on that Chloe and MJ seemed to have their period every nine days.

"So, today is Monday," Annie said. "We'll make your consultation Thursday." She reviewed next year's calendar on her neat desk. "With the New Year's holiday, the committee will meet next Monday and your appointment will be later that day, the first Monday of 1972. Are you still on vacation?"

"Through the first week of January," Chloe said. She wanted to ask, What committee? Annie didn't seem hung up on it, so Chloe decided she wouldn't be either.

"Well, great." Annie handed over a business card for Nathan Thain, MD, and pushed her glasses back up her little nose.

Chloe added the business card to her back pocket, where the soft washcloth was still in residence.

MJ, she saw, gave the uterus a pat-pat before putting it back on its little pedestal.

In the elevator, Chloe fanned herself with her notebook. She checked under her arms—sure enough, pit stains.

"So, uh, how are you going to find a shrink in San Francisco?" MJ asked.

"How do you find the name of anything? The Yellow Pages."

At the pay phone outside the Women's Way, Chloe ran down psychiatrist listings, under *P*, for *physician*. Her finger was sweaty. She smudged the ink. There were thirty-two choices. After eeny-meeny-miny-mo-ing, Chloe landed on Dr. Bernard Glum.

"Nah, that's a bummer name for a doctor," MJ said. "Do you want to see if your aunt's home? She's crazy, right? Maybe she knows a doctor for crazies."

Chloe slid a dime in the coin slot and dialed Kiki. The phone rang seven, eight times. Chloe was about to hang up when she heard a voice, breathless. "Salaam! Marrakesh Express!"

"Aunt Kiki?"

"Who's this?"

"It's Chloe." After a moment of silence, she added, "Chloe Switzer."

"CHLOOOOOE? When are you coming? Tonight? We'll have a grand party when you arrive."

"I'm here. I've been here since yesterday."

"Here? Now? How did that happen?" Kiki sounded like a balloon losing air.

"I tried you a few times last night, but you weren't home."

"Oh, was that you? I was here, but not in a phone-answering frame of mind. Anyway, you're here now, and that's what counts. Come by anytime after four. Or five. Anytime after five."

Chloe called back twice before Kiki answered again and gave her the address, which was around the corner from her old place.

Snoopy time was 8:53. Chloe didn't know what she and MJ would do, rudderless, for another day.

"You didn't ask about a shrink, but it's okay," MJ said with a sideways smile. "Lookee in the phone book again. Inside the cover."

Chloe saw a business card Scotch-taped partially over an ad for Fisherman's Wharf set against a too-orange sunset.

Psychiatrist on Call

Women's Issues a Distinct Specialty

Dr. George Abar

592-5242

Dr. Abar picked up on the first ring and said he had on open slot at one o'clock tomorrow afternoon. Chloe briefly wondered what kind of doctor could see her on a day's notice, but she pushed the thought out of her mind, right over her shoulder.

"I'll take it," Chloe said.

"Please?" he said. "I'll take it, *please*."

"What? Oh," Chloe said, thinking that not a single thing about *This* was easy. "I'll take it, please."

"You're welcome," he said, then *click*.

ROACH-CLIP ORNAMENTS

To kill time, Chloe and MJ went shopping around Union Square. Chloe saw a cute store sign with orange lettering: JUDI'S, with a daisy over the *i*. Banners in the window announced THE UNMATCHABLES COLLECTION! All the clothes were crayon-bright: yellow, green, red, blue.

"Love it!" MJ said, already through the door.

Around and around the racks, MJ grabbed stuff—bolero jackets and plaid pants and mock turtlenecks and jumpers with giant zippers. Her arm buckled under the weight of thirty pieces of clothing.

"Can I put those in a dressing room for you?" a tiny salesgirl asked. She was pretty in an exaggeratedly bright way, like she made puppets on weekends.

Behind the billowy dressing room curtain, MJ loved a pair of elephant bells in corduroy and a sunny marigold tube top she shimmied into position.

Even though Chloe brought in a couple of outfits, she wasn't much in the mood to see herself naked under the fluorescent tubes. She didn't feel fat. She just didn't feel like herself.

Neither of them bought anything, and the tiny salesgirl dropped the bright facade when she didn't make a sale.

Back out on the streets of San Francisco, Chloe and MJ shared a spinach crepe at Magic Pan. They dodged seagulls at the wharf. They peed in the fancy marble bathroom at City Hall.

At five o'clock exactly, they pulled up in front of Kiki's apartment. The new place was a dirty pale green Victorian with a bulging bay window.

Chloe found a parking spot around the corner on Broadway, in front of a large strip club called the Condor. Its neon sign blinked on and off, and a pair of nipples lit the early evening sky. A mustachioed man beckoned ("See the girls or *BE* the girls!"), but they walked by fast.

At the scuffed-up front door of Kiki's apartment, Chloe put down her duffel and rang the bell next to *Kikikiki*.

No one answered.

"You sure this is the place?" MJ asked.

Chloe rang again, leaning hard on the buzzer.

A window opened, and from above Chloe heard Kiki yell, "Heads up!" A balled-up sock landed near MJ's feet. Chloe reached inside and felt fur. A rabbit's foot held a single brass key. She threaded the key into the ancient lock, and the front door heaved open. Chloe and MJ, and their stuff, went up three flights of stairs.

At the top landing, Kiki stood framed by her apartment door. She wore a long-sleeved black Capezio leotard, nothing else. A guy grabbed her from behind and swung her onto his hip in one confident choreographed move. Suddenly they were intertwined—legs knotted, arms entangled. Kiki tipped her head back and laughed. She unwound herself and twirled to give Chloe a hug.

"You look dynamite," Kiki said, leading Chloe into the apartment. MJ followed.

Kiki was the one who looked great. Her blond hair was straight as celery, and her skin was freckled and perfect without makeup. She could have been eighteen—except she was twenty-eight. While MJ was shopping, Chloe had spent time squinting into a circular mirror, brushing on blush and lip gloss and navy blue mascara from the small makeup display. Now she realized she'd tried too hard. She'd missed the beauty boat. Chloe felt a flake of blue drift down her cheek.

"Hey, I'm Fig," the guy said. He seemed older than Kiki, or maybe just tired. He wore a shimmery shirt—it could have been bronze—and had a short ponytail and a long nose.

"Put your stuff anywhere. It's so good you're here," Kiki said. She took Chloe's face in her hands and kissed her on the mouth. "You too! I haven't seen Miss Maryjane since the braces came off." Kiki reached for MJ's face, but MJ dodged out of the way.

"As long as you're here, you can watch our rehearsal," Fig said. "I've been workshopping a short piece."

"Fig teaches over at San Francisco State," Kiki added. "He's helping me transition from modern dance to modern theater."

"We'll perform on New Year's Eve, over at the Nude Relay. We've got four days to create something important and miraculous." He pulled up the kitchen step stool. "Here, take a seat in the audience."

Chloe squished next to MJ on the top step of the stool, the rubber ridges biting into her ass.

"What the hell?" MJ whispered.

Chloe shrugged with her eyes.

From her perch, Chloe checked out Kiki's apartment, surveying the holiday-ness.

Like Chloe, Kiki was officially Jewish, but she'd strung twinkly lights around various ferns and hung a few choice Christmas ornaments—a cable car, a snowman.

"Wait, is that a roach clip?" Chloe gestured to an elf dangling by a metal clasp.

"Brilliant, right?" Kiki said. "Clips for paper! Clips for hair!"

"Hell, I've even worn one as a tie clip to a faculty meeting," Fig said. "Now, let's find some inspirational tunes. . . ."

He fanned out albums from a thousand bands and rattled off the titles. Some Chloe had heard of—Jefferson Airplane, Donovan, the Doors. But most she hadn't—Sopwith Camel, Quicksilver Messenger Service, Fuzzy Duck, Frumious Bandersnatch.

Teddy would die over the unknown bands. He was into music that wasn't on the radio.

"Here's the new Bowie. It's called *Hunky Dory*, but it's pretty kaleidoscopic." Fig put it on the turntable, then knelt in front of a laundry basket.

Kiki draped herself over a rattan chair. Fig handed over a small pile of lingerie. She slipped purple panties over her leotard and stabbed the rest of the underwear around the chair's cushion.

"It's called *Under Where. W-h-e-r-e.* Because we all have things we hide," Kiki said sincerely.

"And . . . action," Fig announced. The record needle dropped.

Kiki slipped out of the panties, pulled on a different pair, and curled in the fetal position.

"Give me that," MJ said in a low voice, pointing to the notebook Chloe still had in her hand from checking Kiki's address.

Chloe passed it over, along with a pen hooked on the front.

Is she ape-shit??? MJ wrote.

Maybe so modern we don't get it? Chloe wrote in teeny-tiny letters.

Mod = Mad?

When the song ended, Kiki stretched up and saluted. She recited a few lines that started like Martin Luther King's "I Have a Dream" speech, which Chloe and MJ had memorized for civics last year.

Kiki had a dream that one day the daughters of housewives would have their underwear—*under where*—ironed by men. She dreamed that one day this nation would WAKE UP! to acknowledge that drugs can be the knives that cut loose the knots of oppression. She dreamed that one day her children would be judged by the coolness of their character rather than by the content of their wallets or the nonsense of their diplomas.

When the scene seemed over, Chloe clapped against her knee, a muffled applause, and said, "Good."

Chin to her chest, Kiki rolled her head like she was working out the kinks.

"Did it speak to you?" Fig asked the girls. "Did you sense the repression?"

"A little," MJ said.

Kiki pulled a billowy skirt over her leotard and pushed through some long wooden beads acting as a curtain to the kitchen. "Would you girls like some cheese? Wait, it's dark. Have you had dinner?" Kiki filled four plastic cups with white wine from a jug and put a box of Frosted Flakes on the table.

"Join us!" Fig offered.

In her current state, Chloe thought the wine smelled like a wet dog. "I'll pass."

"I'll have a few sips," MJ said, downing half the cup in one gulp.

The doorbell buzzed—two short blasts.

Kiki threw open the window. "Well, look at that. There's a cute guy out front," she said to the girls. "Do I know you?" she yelled down.

From two stories below, Chloe heard a familiar voice: "Hey, it's Teddy. MJ's brother."

"Ooooooh . . . who?" Kiki clapped her hands together quickly.

"WHO?" Chloe shot to her feet.

"Teddy!" MJ said, attempting a cheerleader toe-touch but banging into the wall. "He's not even supposed to be in town. How did he know we were here? This night just got better."

MJ stuck her head out the window and yelled, "Did you bring cute friends? Here's a key!" She chucked the rabbit's foot down, sockless.

Chloe felt her heart go out the window with the foot. She grabbed MJ's wrist and headed down the only hall.

"Jesus, what was that for?" MJ asked, shaking her hand free once they were inside a small bathroom.

Chloe glanced around. The tile walls were a murky shade of asparagus green. "Why is he *here*?"

"Hell if I know—it's Teddy. Want to come out with us instead of staying here with your crackers aunt?"

"No, no, no, no. Don't even say I'm here. Say I'm, like, out jogging."

"You don't jog."

"I don't want anybody—*anybody*—to know why I'm here," Chloe said fast.

MJ picked up the tweezers from the side of the sink and went after a stray brow hair. "Believe me, I won't tell, especially not him." She flashed the V sign, for Virgin Mary, which was also the peace sign, which made Chloe wish for a peaceful way out of *This*.

"Just, just . . . just meet him downstairs." Chloe licked her top lip, where little bubbles of sweat were banding together.

"Hey! Hello in there," a voice that belonged to Teddy said on the other side of a not very thick door.

"How did he get up here?" Chloe whisper-shouted.

"Uh, I threw him the key," MJ said.

"Can I come in?" Teddy yelled.

In what she considered a flash of genius, Chloe reached into the shower stall and cranked the hot and cold faucets open. The pipes hissed to life.

Over the pounding of the water, MJ said to Chloe, "If you're worried about your stomach, no one can tell by looking at you. Just say hi. It's just my fucking *brother*."

Teddy opened the door a crack, not enough to stick his head in. "Hey, is Chloe in there, too? Clo?"

"I'm not here." Chloe knew she sounded idiotic.

"Then how come I hear you talking?" Teddy asked, pushing the door open a few more inches.

Chloe yanked back the shower curtain and jumped in. The stall was too small to avoid the showerhead. She centered herself under it and let the water pound.

It felt strange. Strange because what kind of protection was a flimsy shower curtain? Strange because the sound of Teddy's voice, a sound she hadn't heard for four months, could still crack her open. Strange because with her face tilted up, she couldn't tell if it was hot tears or hot water running from her eyes.

On the other side of the plastic was Teddy, whom Chloe had had a great and secret thing with, just short of going all the way, while MJ was away as a camp counselor for the summer. All summer long, Chloe taught the Tadpoles to swim and then sunbathed on the pool deck until Teddy finished lifeguarding. And all summer long, they'd walk to the woods behind the tennis courts and make out until their lips were raw. It was the summer of Yardley Pot o' Gloss. Chloe ran her tongue over her lower lip, trying to taste the memory.

"Chloe is *nuts*," MJ said, apparently to Teddy.

Chloe heard the door click shut. She stayed right there, letting the water slap her clothes against her skin, letting her hair cling to her neck, letting the hot tears or hot water come until she convinced herself that MJ and Teddy were blocks or miles away.

Later, after Chloe had taken a regular shower in the regular naked way, and after she'd put on MJ's Saint Christopher, which she'd grabbed from the ashtray, Kiki rapped on the door. "Chloe, are you okay here alone? We have a party to go to."

"I'm fine." Chloe opened the door, wrapped in a towel. Her clothes were too soaked to put back on.

Kiki, standing in the hallway in front of Fig, took a second to drink in the scene.

"You know, Figgy, party without me," Kiki said, even though she had on a magenta tunic and gold hoops. "I'll hang with Clo."

Chloe didn't protest.

Fig left, and Chloe untied the plastic bag with tomorrow's clothes. By the time she'd gotten dressed, Kiki had made tea.

"I've missed this," Kiki said, handing Chloe a mug filled with chamomile-clove tea.

"Me too," Chloe said, then wondered if Kiki meant her or the tea.

Kiki looked at Chloe longer than most people would. Finally, she said, "What's new? How *are* you?" Kiki put her hand to Chloe's cheek. She wondered if Kiki knew her so inside out she could tell that she needed love anyway, but then she remembered Kiki wasn't even willing to answer the phone last night.

"We've got loads of plans. We're psyched," Chloe said, getting ready to recite her fake tourist itinerary with MJ. She hugged her knees to her chin.

"Are you? Are you sure?"

"Oh, yeah. MJ has never been here. We'll do the wharf, Ghirardelli—"

"Because I observed"—Kiki repositioned herself with her feet tucked under her dancer ass—"that you didn't seem into MJ's surprise visitor. I'm sorry if I made that uncomfortable."

"Am I supposed to know what you're talking about?"

Kiki grinned. "The boy had called here. He was back early from wherever he was. Virginia gave him this number, I guess . . . and I just told him when you'd be here. He sounded fired up about you, and I couldn't resist the wow of a surprise. But you seem a rather sad squirrel." Kiki gently squeezed Chloe's thigh.

"MJ was happy, but Teddy and I . . . we . . ." Chloe looked down at her kneecaps.

"Continue."

Chloe wasn't sure what to tell. Instead she counted. She counted Christmas ornaments on Kiki's ferns, hoping to collect her thoughts along with a little holiday optimism.

There were twenty-three things hanging from the ferns. Chloe said, "Teddy and I were together last summer. Together-together. But MJ doesn't know. She can't know. Please, Kiki, please don't tell her."

"I'm mum. I'm a mummy." Kiki reached over and ran her fingers through Chloe's curls, like she used to a million years ago when Chloe was trying to master the mysteries of the French braid. "Was he a good kisser?"

"Kiki!"

"Oh, is that gauche? I mean, a good kisser is hard to find."

"Yes, but we broke up, and I was with this other guy." Chloe frowned. "Not such a good kisser. And all I can think since is I, uh, kissed the wrong guy. So to speak."

"You know what makes a good kiss?" Kiki asked. "The spirit. It should be experimental, passionate, uninhibited." Kiki swayed to some imaginary music. "Don't you think?"

Chloe allowed herself to think about Teddy's kisses for a second. They were all of the above. "It doesn't matter. Maybe the next guy's kisses were just wrong."

Kiki took a long draw of tea and swung her eyes toward the ceiling. "I hate to see you hung up. So I have a brilliant little idea." She stood and unpretzeled. "Let's put your feelings in a box."

"I've been doing that. Pushing them down."

"And does that help you? I think not. You need a real box, like a cigar box." Kiki opened the oven, where there were several boxes of different sizes. "Take this one."

Chloe flipped up the top: empty.

"Good, keep it open. Pour in your heart—the kisses, the memories, the love. Did you make love to him?"

Chloe shook her head. No, she didn't make love to him, but she also couldn't believe what a nut Kiki was.

"Okay, the lovemaking stays out. Transport your feelings, and I'll get the sage."

While Kiki untied a bundle of dried herbs hanging over the kitchen sink, Chloe looked around for an actual something to put in the box. Kiki might believe in the abstract, but Chloe liked the world of the tangible. Without overthinking it, she reached into her back pocket and extracted the washcloth-lovey from the German boy. She nestled it in the box, a childlike souvenir for a big-girl problem.

Using an abalone shell as an ashtray, Kiki was back with a bundle of lit sage. She waved the sage over each of the box's four corners and then closed the lid and smudged some ash in the center.

"For the record," Kiki said, "I believe in the power of love. I'm not really into denying feelings. So. I'm sort of rooting for this not to work."

Chloe kissed the box good-bye, careful not to get her lips near the sage smudges, which reeked like bad weed.

She put the box back in the cold oven, knowing that because of *This*, no matter how she felt about Teddy, she'd have to root for the opposite. She'd have to root against love.

STICKY FINGERS

For a while, Chloe waited up for MJ, but she didn't show. After Fig stumbled in with a sloppy one-finger salute, Chloe fell asleep curled up, like a comma, on the velvet window seat. The velvet was musty, and its cushion wasn't cushy, but Chloe wanted to stay as far away as possible from Kiki's bedroom. Since Fig had come back, there were wave-making sounds coming from the waterbed.

Around eight in the morning, the phone rang, and Chloe lunged for it before the *bring* woke the aqua couple.

"Hi ho!" MJ said from the other end of the line, all chipper.

"Ugh, hold on." Standing up made Chloe queasy. She put the receiver down and booked it to the green bathroom to make one, then two deposits. While she was toilet-side, Chloe found herself staring at the grout on the floor. It was a swampy black. Kiki probably hadn't scrubbed the floor since she'd moved in. Chloe flushed and rubbed her knees. She wanted to brush, but she didn't want MJ to hang up, so she squirted a shot of toothpaste on her tongue and ran back to the phone.

"Okay, back. Where are you?"

"Don't freak. Berkeley, with Teddy. His roommate is a fox. We have this connection, like a spiritual thing." MJ giggled in one long trill.

The toothpaste was so minty it burned.

"Will you be here soon?" Chloe asked, trying to swallow the remnants of the toothpaste and a slight feeling of desertion. "I've got that appointment—"

"I know, I'm coming. Don't go all bat-shit on me, though, because Teddy is driving me back."

"No! NO!" Chloe frantically shook her head, even though MJ couldn't see her. "Don't. Don't do that."

"You worried me last night, Clo. You can't duck in the shower like some psycho. You've got to be out there in the world." MJ was talking too loudly. "I've been up all night, and I've got to crash because I see prisms inside my eyelids. But you and Teddy go and have coffee without me. He says he wants to talk to you about school."

Chloe breathed in deep, twice. "He said that? The thought of coffee makes me want to puke about now."

"So have tea. I'm looking out for you, trust me." MJ hung up.

It seemed to Chloe that anyone who said "trust me" was not trustworthy. Nixon said "trust me" about Vietnam. Virginia said "trust me" about Chloe's dad coming back. Shep said "trust me" about the condom.

Out the window, the sun was bright, but inside Chloe's head, there was fog. She'd lost track of the logic that had her keep the Teddy thing from MJ in the first place. It was easy at first—MJ was gone all summer, a camp counselor up the canyon, and anyway, she and Teddy had figured they'd be history by the time MJ got back. Actually, Teddy didn't care that much. It was Chloe who was hung up on the idea that he was either MJ's brother or Chloe's boyfriend, not both. And anyway, by the time MJ was home Teddy was gone, and Chloe had chosen to misremember the summer into nothing.

The phone rang again.

"You're up!" Virginia's voice came through loud and clear. "You didn't call yesterday. Tell me what's shaking. A liberated attitude on my part does not mean utter freedom for you."

"Hello, Virginia." Chloe thought of the Women's Way and the phone booth and Fig and the oven of love. "Yesterday was kind of . . . strange."

Virginia was momentarily quiet. Chloe imagined she was on the verge of meditating. "Well, strange can be interesting. In fact, I have a new friend, but he's not so strange. I wanted to let you know. While you're having an adventure, so am I. He's Stan. Stan from the university. He's evolved, psychologically speaking, and very well proportioned."

"Virginia, please."

The sound of her mother's voice made Chloe queasy all over again. Or maybe it was what her mother had to say. She didn't want to hear about Stan, whoever Stan was. Or imagine what Virginia and Stan might be doing. Last month, after an awareness-building weekend, Virginia shared a tip for achieving a mind-blowing orgasm. Apparently, it had to do with lifting the legs up and over the head.

It didn't exactly encourage Chloe to share anything about her own encounter, singular. Who would want to compare sex notes with a mother who was continually honing her craft? Especially since Chloe hadn't been wowed by the experience. She'd hoped it would be sweeter, somehow.

"Anyway, Stan and I saw a report on Walter Cronkite last night about bad mushrooms sending kids in San Francisco to the hospital. If someone offers you mushrooms—"

"No mushrooms," Chloe agreed. The thought of fungi, hallucinogenic or sautéed, made her stomach roil. Or maybe it was Virginia. Chloe tried to remember what it was like to have a mother who kept her sexual proclivities to herself.

"Mom, I've got to go."

"Virginia! It's *Virginia*. . . ."

The door to Kiki's room was still shut. Chloe went back into the bathroom to shower again, even though she wasn't dirty. Her hair looked mystifyingly bad. Other people liked Chloe's curls, but they didn't know what a major hassle it was to work the shampoo in, out, back, and around all those ringlets.

It was weird how an ugly bathroom could make a person feel worse. Under the sink, Chloe found a sponge and, once the water was scalding hot, alternately scrubbed herself with a loofah and the shower with the sponge.

Somewhere between rinse and repeat, while her fingers massaged her skull, her brain came up with a good idea. She'd deal with Teddy head-on. See him and be done with it, face him instead of running, act instead of reacting. It was the mature thing to do and, even if she didn't feel mature standing in the shower where she'd taken shelter fully-clothed last night, it was a state to aspire to.

By the time Chloe turned off the shower, both she and the tile seemed cleaner and clearer.

It wasn't even nine o'clock.

At ten, Kiki stumbled into the kitchen to make coffee, hair in a bird's nest.

"Do you want breakfast?" Kiki asked.

"I made toast."

"Toast? I don't have a toaster," Kiki said.

"I used the oven. Don't worry about the boxes. I took them out." Chloe pointed to the top of the refrigerator, where the cigar box and its friends sat. "I don't think the box theory is working anyway, because Teddy is on his way over."

"Aha," Kiki said, playfully slapping the oven handle. "Maybe I'm right."

Maybe Kiki's favorite word was *maybe*.

Before Chloe could disagree, the buzzer rang.

Without looking out the window, Kiki said, "Go on, throw a foot."

A basket by the window held dozens of rabbit feet—pink, purple, tie-dye, red-ombré, black, bittersweet orange—some with keys, some naked. Chloe picked the one neutral color, a sandy gray, opened the window, and let it fly.

MJ bolted up the stairs. For a minute, Chloe thought Teddy had bailed, but no. "Good, you're dressed. Teddy's downstairs. Talk to him about college. You applied to Berkeley—he's at Berkeley. That should be enough for an hour of talk." MJ yawned, exposing a ribbon of fillings.

"What did you tell him?"

"That you wigged out. Don't worry, I didn't tell him the

knocked-up part," MJ said, whispering the last few words. "Me, I'm gonna crash."

Chloe grabbed her scarf and slunk down the stairs. Teddy was leaning against a telephone pole, his face tilted up to catch rays.

Chloe had forgotten, in the four months since they'd last seen each other, how cute he was. Tall sexy, smart sexy, funny sexy, sexy sexy.

"Hey." For a second Chloe thought he was going to shake her hand.

"Hey." Chloe double-wrapped her scarf around her neck. MJ's older sister, Peg, had crocheted it for her in all these shades of purple.

"Want to walk?"

"Not really." Chloe inhaled, willing her stomach to pull in line with her jeans rather than revealing the merest suggestion of *This*.

"C'mon!" He started walking, then turned and walked backward, waiting for Chloe to catch up. He had MJ's dark hair, longer now, sort of Paul McCartney, though Chloe preferred Lennon.

"Things are fine," Chloe said to a question Teddy hadn't asked.

At a tiny coffee place a few blocks away, they sat at a wobbly table by the window. A small sign said COFFEE AS BITTER AS LIFE.

Teddy ordered espresso. Chloe asked for a Coca-Cola, but the waitress with thighs like Pixy Stix shook her head.

"Have an espresso," Teddy suggested.

"I don't like coffee." Which he'd known at one point, Chloe added in her head.

"Espresso is different."

The drinks came in dwarf cups. Teddy pleated his lips and took a draw. "So how's life back in Phoenix?"

"Same," Chloe said. She wished.

"I don't miss the sun. I was up in Sacramento and it rained all week."

It was sad to have known someone so well, Chloe thought, to have had them under your skin all summer, and then find yourself talking about the weather. They'd broken up—on the phone, on a sunny day—before Teddy took off. "Makes sense, right?" he'd said. "New people, new places." Chloe hadn't wanted to say what she'd really thought, which was simply: not for me. In the four months since they'd seen each other, he'd written exactly once, a letter full of college bullshit.

She tried a sip of espresso. "Uh! I don't get it."

"Get what?"

"The coffee. It's gross."

"That's what's great about you," Teddy said. "You don't pretend."

There was silence while Teddy sipped and Chloe stared out the window at the City Lights bookstore. She once spent hours there with Virginia, nose-deep in used children's books. *Elsie Dinsmore, Elsie's Holidays, Elsie's Girlhood.* How great would it be to thumb through the pages of her childhood. She twirled the Saint Christopher around and around her thumb.

"Hey, is that MJ's necklace?"

"Uh, yeah." Chloe swallowed. "I got to go, I don't want to ditch MJ for long."

Teddy put his little cup down. "I was kind of psyched to see you.

You know, why not say it? I've missed you. But here you are, and you don't seem psyched to see me."

For a wild second, Chloe thought about going with the truth. She imagined saying: "I made a mistake." Or the longer version: "I'm pregnant. I made a mistake." She looked at Teddy, into his brown eyes, searching for a sign that she should spill.

But Teddy kept talking. "MJ says you've been hanging with Shep. That kid who flips his hair around."

That stopped Chloe's musings. "MJ said that? What else did she tell you?" Chloe waited a beat before she looked up again and stuck a so-what smile on her face. "And, anyway, what do you care? We broke up."

He shrugged. "I care."

Chloe shrugged back, but then she slumped a little because she cared, too. "I made a mistake," she added out loud, but not loudly. Her thumb, still wrapped around MJ's necklace, stretched the chain too far, and it broke, puddling into her palm.

"Shit, shit," Chloe said, pinching the clasp back together.

"Want me to put that back on you?"

"No!" The thought of Teddy's nice fingers on her skin, her neck, made Chloe cringe.

"Touchy," Teddy said. "Shep always seemed"—he knocked on the little table—"hollow. Nothing's there."

"*Something's* there," Chloe said fast. Even if she wanted to forget that afternoon, it was there. And now *This* was there.

And Teddy was here.

"Good for you." Teddy picked up his cup and swirled it.

"Right, good for me." Chloe could feel tears start to well up, but she wasn't sure why. Her brain was flipping stations. She wasn't thinking about Shep. She was remembering how it felt to kiss Teddy, his hands against her face.

"Okay, then." Teddy left two bucks on the table, and Chloe wrapped her scarf tight around her neck. When they got out on the street, Teddy asked, "So have you heard Boz Scaggs? He's a local guy with this great Mussel Shoals sound."

Chloe considered pretending so she could get back to Kiki's, but she didn't need to lie about that. She shook her head.

"Then you can't go yet. To understand about San Francisco you need to understand about the twelve-minute track 'Loan Me a Dime.' Everyone's got that glued to the turntable. Well, that's a line from a *Rolling Stone* review, but it's true."

Chloe was reminded of how honest and good Teddy was.

And the guy had good taste in music. That was another thing.

Teddy matched his pace to Chloe's, stride for stride, even though he was a foot taller. Walking where no one knew them, two people in a private world, Chloe thought they looked like a couple. Why not? Chloe was super aware of her clothes against her body, the drips of sweat on the back of her neck under her scarf. From her back pocket, Chloe took out a leather stick barrette and twisted her hair into a bun.

There it was, on the corner of Bay and Columbus: a giant yellow and red sign for Tower Records, the letters leaning backward like they were too wasted to stand up. A smaller sign, hand-lettered, announced:

Largest Record Store in the Known World
Open 9 'til Midnight 365 days a Year!

Teddy held the door open for Chloe. "It's the real place. DJs come here. Music freaks. Everyone."

It took a second for her eyes to adjust from the baked sunlight of the street to Tower's cave. She breathed in. It smelled like old books.

Prices dangled from mobiles hung low from the ceiling. THE FLYING BURRITO BROTHERS, $3.88. TODD RUNDGREN, $4.88. The place must have had every record ever pressed: comedy, classical, soul, rockabilly, baroque, and rock. A football field of rock.

"Cool, right?" Teddy asked. He pulled out a pale album called, not too cleverly, *ZZ Top's First Album,* and spun it around. "Want to start at *Z*?"

"Nah," Chloe said, wanting to turn Teddy off, to turn down his volume and also turn off her own interest in his tall self, even though he was a music guy. Over the summer he'd introduced her to British bootlegs. She had never given back a scratchy single recorded at Wimbledon of the Who's "Baba O'Riley." The song wasn't called "Teenage Wasteland" *(Don't cryyyyyy, don't raise an eye. It's only teeeeenage wastelaaand).* Everyone thought it was, but because of Teddy, Chloe knew better.

Chloe left Teddy by one of the little listening booths and snaked down the aisles, past *Z Y X W V* on her way to the *A* bin. She flipped past Aaron Neville, Al Green, Alice Cooper, to the Allman Brothers Band. At first it messed with Chloe's disciplined disposition to see the albums alphabetized erratically—by first name, last name, band name, all together. But then she let it go, because she needed to learn to let stuff go.

It was weird that ten minutes ago in the coffee shop she was fixated on the bad—avoiding Teddy's eyes, obsessing about *This*—and yet here she was smiling and humming in spite of herself.

Maybe that's what San Francisco did to people. Made them happy against the evidence.

Halfway through the *C* bin, Chloe checked out Creedence Clearwater Revival; the store had all six albums, including the first one, which she remembered was hard to find. A guy who could have been CCR's John Fogerty was at her elbow.

It probably wasn't him, but it could have been. That was the point, the possibility of it all. All her fellow browsers looked like they led exciting or at least colorful lives—embroidered jeans, ponchos, lace-up granny boots. Chloe tried to telepathically borrow some of their self-belief.

Teddy was out of view, but Chloe felt stronger, less seesaw-y. She picked up the new Rolling Stones album, *Sticky Fingers*. The cover had a zipper, an actual zipper, bulging over a well-packed crotch.

Chloe unzipped it a little. It worked.

And then Teddy was back. He was a little sticky himself, a little hard to forget, to wash off.

"We're here for a reason," he said, swinging a yellow Tower bag in one hand and leading her with the other. She wanted to drop his hand, really she did. But she didn't. He steered her into a listening booth, almost like a pay phone except with less glass and less air.

Teddy slipped an album out of the bag and palmed the record. The needle dropped on a track on side B. He reached for a pair of headphones hanging from a nail and handed them to Chloe. "Listen."

She did.

Chloe didn't know if it was the music (twelve minutes of this great whiskey-gravel voice) or the lyric (*Somebody loan me a dime, I need to calllll my old time*) or the shared air (Teddy's exhales became Chloe's inhales), but there, in that private, soundproof booth, in that minute, hip to hip with Teddy, Chloe had the spark of hope that maybe she wasn't pregnant and maybe she would kiss Teddy.

"Unbelievable," Chloe said in the scratchy silence between tracks.

Teddy took off her headphones. "That was Duane Allman on the slide guitar."

"A lot has happened since you left," Chloe said, her eyes closed.

"Uh-huh." Teddy ran his thumb down her cheek.

Chloe opened her eyes to see Teddy bending in for a kiss.

At the moment of contact, his lips were soft and warm like sunshine or a tortilla.

Then, *boom boom boom,* a guy with a purple bandanna around his head jerked into the booth. "Hey, man. Your turn is up!"

That rocketed Chloe back to now, to *This* reason she was really in San Francisco. She walked out of the booth, walked right out of the store, and kept walking down Bay Street in what she hoped was the direction of the glittering, sequined bay.

It might have been unnecessarily dramatic, but it felt like she was *doing* something.

She didn't get more than two blocks before Teddy was at her heels. "What's going on with you?"

He took hold of her scarf and spun her back to him, like some modern dance move Kiki might make up.

"I've got stuff to do," Chloe said, snatching her scarf back.

On the curb, a girl who looked a few years younger than Chloe offered to take a picture of Chloe and Teddy for a dime. "Loan Me a Dime"—Chloe would never look at dimes the same way again. A Polaroid camera hung, limp and sad, around the girl's neck. Her hair was dirty.

"I don't have a picture of you," Teddy said.

"Good," Chloe said under her breath.

Teddy dug in his pocket for a handful of change, then threw his arm around Chloe, out of habit, she guessed.

"Did I screw up?" Teddy whispered into Chloe's ear.

The girl pressed the button, and the image spit out of the Polaroid's mouth.

Even though she wanted to bolt, Chloe stayed, transfixed, and watched the picture develop. Her face appeared first, misty, as if she was living in a puddle. They were oddly matched, height-wise. The top of her head was level with his shoulder. Teddy looked great—he and his nice eyes. In that moment, seeing an outside-in view of the two of them side by side, a pair, a duo, she had an urge to kiss him. Again.

"So what now?" Teddy asked, slipping the Polaroid into his back pocket. Chloe hoped it wouldn't get bent, but then she told herself she didn't care.

Now? Now she had to boogie over to the psychiatrist. "You go back to your life, and I go back to mine."

It wasn't what she'd wanted to say, but that was the new now.

UPSIDE-DOWN DUCKS

MJ piloted the Lady Bug over to Chinatown, past the Italian delis and the old guys practicing tai chi in the park, without a word about her brother. Chloe took that as two good signs—that MJ was sort of supporting *This*, and she wasn't suspicious of That, aka Teddy.

The psychiatrist's office was up a shaky staircase, on the third floor of a jade jewelry emporium. From a window on the landing, Chloe and MJ had a bird's-eye view of Chinatown over the pagoda roofs and dragon lampposts.

"Chinese writing looks sort of like Hebrew, except not really," Chloe said, looking down at the store flags unfurled.

"I like the red and gold, gold and red," MJ said. "But this place is a dump."

There was no waiting room, no swively secretary. Just a dark hallway and a wood door with ABAR, MD imprinted on a flimsy plaque, like he was too cheap to even add his first name.

Chloe knocked.

Dr. Abar cracked the door open. Chloe could see his nose. "I'm with an appointment. Running a little late," he said. Then *click*, the door shut, and it was just Chloe, MJ, and the sad hallway again.

MJ hung her head upside down, shook, and asked, "Does this setup remind you of those sex-ed filmstrips in eighth grade?" She flipped back up and her hair fell into place with more fluff.

"Nope." But Chloe's brain flashed on a blurry filmstrip anyway, called something like *Prized Life*. Or *Life Is a Prize*. As the filmstrip flickered, a narrator talked about a "wanton woman" using a knitting needle to end a pregnancy. Chloe closed her eyes to erase the image, but the reel kept playing inside her head.

The doctor opened the door. No one walked out.

"Come in, come in," Dr. Abar said, rubbing both hands over his bald head like he was his own Magic 8-Ball. He motioned to a nubby couch.

The girls sat close together.

"Tell me, young ladies, what can I do for you? Is it both of you?"

"It's me," Chloe said, moving to the edge of the sofa. "I'm pregnant, and I didn't intend to be." She wished there was a desk or something to lean against.

"A familiar predicament. This is a role I've played with many girls in the same position as yourself. Want my advice?"

"Yes, I do," Chloe said, exhaling with relief that this doctor knew his stuff. After a second, she added, "But I also want, or need, I guess, your permission." She felt in control, at attention.

"Let's discuss how far along you are and what options you have considered," the doctor said.

MJ stood up, stretched, and walked over to an aquarium so cloudy with algae it was hard to tell if anything lived inside.

"Five weeks, or perhaps six. And I've decided on the option." Chloe wondered if there was a secret code word she was supposed to use. "The option of abortion."

Dr. Abar crossed his arms and let the room get quiet.

"It is my obligation to inform you," he said, "that an abortion can pose a risk to young women. I want to make sure you're aware of all the dangers."

"I am. I'm willing to take the risk," Chloe said with adopted confidence.

"And what of the young man? How does he feel?"

"Ha!" MJ said. "Class-A jerk." The doctor didn't even turn his head toward her.

"He approves, but I'm not sure why that is . . . relevant," Chloe said.

"Ah, it's all relevant. Have you been to New York, New York?" Dr. Abar asked.

Chloe shook her head.

"My hometown," the doctor volunteered.

"I'm from Arizona." Chloe wondered what the point was. Maybe shrinks had to shrink normal conversation down to these tiny bits of information to judge whether a person was sane or not.

Dr. Abar smoothed back his nonexistent hair. "New York is THE abortion mecca. They have the most liberal laws in the country. Colleagues there tell me they have to run shuttles to the airports to pick up gals who fly in from Columbus or Sheboygan . . ."

From her research Chloe also knew there was something called the Jane Collective in Chicago, where U Chicago students did abortions on one another, and they'd performed twelve thousand so far. But she was here, not there. What did there matter?

The light in the room shifted. A diagonal shaft of sun crossed the carpet, striping it yellow, a sudden colossal beach umbrella.

"Yes," Chloe said after a minute, though she'd lost track of the conversation. Maybe she should have said no.

"My point is, and there is one . . ." Dr. Abar seemed amused with himself. "My point is that a young lady has many options. You don't seem, in my medical estimation, to be in any imminent danger from the pregnancy. You seem certifiably sane. The great state of California allows the false risk to the health of the mother to take precedence over the real life of the unborn."

Chloe was lost.

He looked right at her. "Do you know the first rule of medicine?"

"I don't." Chloe sensed she was in for a lecture.

"The first rule is 'Do no harm.' I cannot give you what you want. You look in good health. An abortion is an *elective* procedure. Therefore I recommend you *elect* not to do it."

The doctor's words swam by, and Chloe tried to catch the ones that seemed crucial. *I cannot give you what you want.* That seemed crucial.

"Thanks for your opinion—" Chloe started to say.

"I am not finished." The doctor stood up and walked over to Chloe. She stood up, too, not wanting to be looked down on.

"You will likely find a different psychiatrist who will give you what you want, but you will also have to ask your parent for her or his blessing. You will have to face the music. I hope you also face the consequences."

"I will." Chloe wanted her voice to be stronger, surer, but she tripped over his smug delivery of *consequences*. Wasn't that what she was doing?

"She's *already* facing them," MJ threw in. "That's why we're here."

"That will be fifteen dollars. Cash or check," Dr. Abar said.

"Don't pay, Clo," MJ said. "What kind of help is he?"

Chloe considered stiffing him, but then she'd be playing dirty, too. She opened her wallet and took out three five-dollar bills, representing thirty hours' worth of babysitting the Wood kids.

With each clomp of the stairs, Chloe's mood sank. By the time she and MJ got down all three flights, she was forty-two steps depressed.

"What an assnick," MJ said, playing with her necklace.

"I was thinking Kiki must have a phone book," Chloe said, imagining the Saint Christopher with the squished-together clasp snapped into her wallet. Maybe she should take it out for air.

"What if someone is trying to tell us something? To reconsider?" MJ asked. "I think I should pray on it."

Chloe pivoted on her heel. "I'm open to all help, but maybe leave the fact that I'm Jewish out of the prayer."

"Are you making fun of me?" MJ gnawed her lip. "I can't tell."

"I'm not, you crazy little nun." When they were younger, MJ thought she wanted to be a nun. That was before she discovered boys and blow jobs.

"Yeah, guess this'll get in the way of the nunnery," MJ said.

"A few other things got in the way, Our Lady of BJs." Chloe laughed.

MJ laughed too. "I haven't done anything that can't be cleansed by confession. Ah, confession!"

They walked a few blocks in search of food. The first three

restaurants they passed had rows, rows, rows of those upside-down Chinese ducks, plucked and shriveled and very dead. The sight of the naked flesh made Chloe nearly hyperventilate.

"Don't freaking faint," MJ said. "Stay here, and I'll acquire."

Chloe stared in the window of a fabric store with bolts of silk standing upright, red and cobalt and emerald. Chloe wished for a world of saturated happy colors, where self-righteous doctors didn't trick girls, and ducks destined to be restaurant fare swam free, and girls who had plans for themselves weren't stupid enough to get pregnant.

MJ returned with lo mein takeout in one hand and balled-up rosary beads in the other.

"Where did you get those?" Chloe asked.

"These?" MJ fingered the beads. "Bottom of my bag. My mom stuck them in there for a rainy day. I had to pick off the lint."

They sat on one of the steps under the copper-green pagoda on Grant Street, passing the carton back and forth, stabbing it with chopsticks.

"So a little girl tells a nun she wants to be a prostitute," MJ said.

"Is this a joke?"

"Duh. And the nun says, 'What did you say?' "

"And?"

"And the little girl repeats that she wants to be a prostitute. And the nun says, 'Oh, thank God! I thought you said you want to be a Protestant.' "

"Thanks," Chloe said.

MJ smiled wide. "The nuns say you're welcome."

SLIDING DOWN CONCRETE

Soy-sauced up, Chloe revved the Bug. She didn't feel like going back to Kiki's place and looking through the Yellow Pages. The thought of that big phone book with thin pages and itty-bitty type was bumming her out. And she didn't want to think about finky Dr. Abar, but she couldn't stop herself. It was like the hairline crack she had in her windshield last spring. The crack spidered up and out until it threatened to shatter the whole glass.

She stuffed her foot down on the clutch and put the Bug in neutral. "Hey, MJ, I don't know why I'm about to say this, but—"

"Shit, Clo. What now?"

"No, this you'll like, I think. Before I have to be a grown-up, do you want to spin back to kindergarten days? Play in the park?" Chloe asked.

"Hell, yeah." Play and MJ were always friends. "But don't you need to find a doctor *today*?"

"Tomorrow. I still have two days before the consultation."

"Two tomorrows."

From a few visits ago, Chloe remembered that Golden Gate Park had a great swing set by the old carousel. She drove up and over Nob Hill and snaked her way over to Geary, stalling only once. Chloe parked on the street near the Japanese Gardens, and they got out.

There were kids at the playground, but there were Kiki types, too, young women with long hair and long skirts and the occasional feather-plumed hat, dazing around. The wind had kicked up, and the swings pushed themselves back and forth, like they were powered by invisible children.

"I need a Tab," MJ announced.

Chloe had spent so much time in her head, she couldn't wait to run, climb, swing, and slide. She gave MJ quick directions to the concession stand she remembered by the carousel, and skipped over to the two-story concrete slide with a giant hump-bump in the middle.

At the top of the slide, a boy with a missing front tooth played ringmaster. He handed Chloe a piece of cardboard to sit on for added speed.

Chloe took off, arms high in victory, closing her eyes to the slide show, her own private View-Master, of summer images past: turtle sandbox, cherry Icees, underwater handstands, a jar of cocoa butter liquefying in the afternoon heat, tequila sunrises, Teddy.

Over at the swings, Chloe grabbed the chains holding the swing to the frame and slung her ass in. She kicked her legs hard, really hard, getting off on the idea that there was no external force driving her higher, just her own power. Eyes closed, head back, she willed herself to go as high as physics would allow, pumping in rhythm to the song "Cecilia," because she loved singing the word *jub-i-la-tion*. There was no way to say *jubilation* without smiling.

When Chloe finally slowed down and looked to her right, she saw a mother holding a baby in her lap two swings over.

"Hiiii!" The baby waved to Chloe. She was wearing a red corduroy jacket and matching beret.

"Hi!" Chloe waved back.

The mother was young and wore tiny pearl earrings and overalls. She whispered into the baby's ear, and the baby threw Chloe a kiss, then more kisses, one after another, with her chubby fist.

Chloe pretended to catch the kisses, which was a pointless thing to do, because she was still swinging, a moving target.

The mother, her arms wrapped casually around the little girl's waist, rocked just a little.

"How old is she?" Chloe asked as she scraped her feet in the dirt to slow down.

"Almost a year," the mother said, brushing the girl's bangs off her forehead.

A year, Chloe thought. Wow. In a year and seven months, that could be her, except it wouldn't.

The baby giggled, giggled, giggled and then scrunched her eyes, looked to the sky, and let out a cosmically loud cry. Her red beret fell off.

"Oh, lovey," the mother said, scooping up the hat and reaching into the front pocket of her overalls to pull out an amber pacifier.

The baby spit it into the mother's hand and wailed.

The mother gave the pacifier back.

"Hola!" MJ reappeared, Tab in hand. "Let's sit on the grass."

Chloe waved bye to the baby, who spit out her pacifier again, this time into the dirt.

In one graceful motion, MJ grabbed the pacifier, blew on it, once, then twice, and handed it back to the mom. "One-second rule."

"Bye, bye," the baby said as they walked away.

On a gentle hill overlooking the playground, MJ knelt down, without checking to see if the grass was wet. It was. "So here's the story," she said, repeating the first line of the *Brady Bunch* song, even though they hated the show.

"What story?" Chloe asked, squatting and teetering on her clogs so her butt didn't get wet.

MJ nodded in the direction of the now-empty swings, then bent her head. Chloe couldn't see her face but heard a low, melodic murmur. It took a few minutes before Chloe caught on: MJ was praying.

MJ lifted her head for air. "Hail Mary, full of grace, the Lord is with thee. . . ." And she was down again. Then up. "And blessed is the fruit of thy womb, Jesus." Then down.

The prayer got faster each time MJ said it. For fifteen minutes, MJ worked over the beads, her fingers going faster, her words softer, little hiccups of prayer.

Chloe watched, aching. She braided and unbraided and rebraided her hair.

When MJ was done, she lay back in the grass with a beatific smile.

"Was all that for me?" Chloe whispered.

"Not you." MJ sat up. "I'm praying for your being. It has a soul."

Chloe gnawed on her upper lip. "There's no soul in four cells."

"In case there is. . . . I saw you there with that kid in the swing, and I thought, you know, my mom didn't *plan* to have Eliza. She and Dad were all through with us kids and then this baby joined us. And now Eliza is the best part of the family. What will you be missing? What if you regret it?"

Chloe sucked in a breath. Of course she'd regret it. How could she not? She thought back to a few weekends ago when she'd biked over to MJ's. Eliza was up, wearing footy pj's and swinging a Barbie by its oddly arched feet. "Go ahead, pull!" Eliza said. Under Barbie's mock turtle was a string. Chloe tugged. "What should I wear to the prom?" Barbie asked as the cord retracted into her back. Then "Let's have a fashion show!" Was that what MJ meant? The feeling Chloe had when Eliza was nestled in her lap, warm and light, her hair smelling like Johnson's tear-free shampoo?

MJ flung her head forward over her stretched-out legs, like she was doing the sit-and-reach.

"I know you're right," Chloe said. "But I know . . . well, I don't know. I hope. I hope I'm right, too."

MJ's head came up.

Chloe went on. "Because it's not just *This*. It's also me. *This* is a dot, and I'm a whole person." She stood up and stretched her arms overhead.

MJ tore at the grass, plucking a few pieces from the ground, splitting them down the middle, and making a pile of broken blades. "I was all jokey an hour ago, but something's different."

In a park with many people, Chloe felt lonely.

"Maybe it's that kid with the pacifier," MJ went on. "Or the Hail Marys. Or thinking of Eliza."

"So, what, you've changed your mind?" Chloe asked.

"I just can't go to those appointments with you." MJ's eyes were wet. "I'll drive you, but I can't hear what they tell you inside anymore."

The fog rolled in like a wet blanket. It was time to move on.

When the girls got home, Fig was back at the apartment and Kiki wasn't. He wore a thin white shirt embroidered with silver thread. Metallic seemed to be his thing. Chloe wondered which side of thirty he was on; he looked older but acted younger.

"Can I interest you in a little Maui Wowie?" he asked, lighting up a fat joint. "Or a tour of the Haight? We can blast by the Janis house. The Charlie Manson house. We knew him long before he stabbed the pretty actress people."

"Not for me," Chloe said, stepping out of her clogs by the front door. Even before *This*, Chloe didn't like to smoke. She had tried once, watching the joint make the rounds, studying the rhythm of puff-puff-pass. When her turn came, Chloe took the joint in her fingers, but she didn't bring it close enough to her mouth and choked on air. Worse, she handed the joint back to the girl on her right. "Hey, bonehead," said a water-polo player who'd just joined the circle, "joints move clockwise."

Fig took a long drag. "You looked wiped out, Chloe-Q. Anything I can do? You need a shot of something? Whatever you need, I can find. Want tickets to the Stones? Want strawberry milk? Want a shrink to get your boyfriend out of the draft? Want a line on the Super Bowl? I'm Fig the Fixer."

"Does Kiki have a phone book?" Chloe asked.

"Hey, do you really know a good shrink, not just for boyfriends but for girlfriends?" MJ asked. She wiggled her brows in Chloe's direction.

Chloe shook her head. "Don't," she stage-whispered to MJ. "Not if you don't want to."

"This part," MJ said, "I can do." To Fig, she continued. "We have this *friend*. She needs a San Francisco–type doctor. Long hair. Liberal."

"She's screwed." To Chloe's surprise, her voice broke, halfway between a hiccup and a sob.

"Well, then. Let's unscrew her." Fig levitated off the futon. He dug into his front jeans pocket, pulling out an assortment of cash, crumpled receipts, and scraps of paper. "Here." He flicked a creased business card in Chloe's direction. "This is Dr. Feelgood's number. His actual name is Dr. Reed, and he's legit. Anyone who needs a shrink, call this guy and tell him Fig sent you."

"Thanks," Chloe said, rubbing her arms at high speed, a little self-hug.

While Fig took MJ for a Hashbury tour and Kiki was wherever, Chloe stayed at the apartment alone. She took down the cigar box from the top of the refrigerator and put it back in the oven. It would be great if she could wait a few minutes then check on her box of feelings for Teddy like they were cupcakes. She wished she could pierce them with a toothpick and see if they were done.

Instead, Chloe dialed Fig's doctor.

"Reed here."

"Oh. Dr. Reed?" She had been expecting a secretary. "Hi, you don't know me. My name is Chloe Switzer, and I—"

"Hi, Chloe Switzer."

"I was given your number by Fig . . ." Chloe realized she didn't know Fig's last name. "Fig the Fixer."

He laughed. "Any friend of Fig's . . ."

Dr. Reed must have really owed Fig, because there was the briefest volley of conversation before he agreed to see Chloe at eight the next morning.

After a day of noise, Chloe curled into the window seat and let the silence fill her head. When MJ returned a few hours later, sans Fig, she had a tie-dye tank top, some tinkly elephant bells from India, and a glaze in her eyes that wasn't ceramic. So they had both gotten some of what they wanted.

SUNSHINE TENNIS BALL

"**G**ood morning, starshine," Kiki said, coming out of the bedroom and into the kitchen, where Chloe and MJ were considering the pantry. "Starshines, plural, I guess." Kiki wore a button-down shirt from a guy who must have been taller than Fig. "I'm craving goat curry for breakfast, how about you? I'm considering getting a goat and keeping it up in Marin for the milk."

"No thanks," Chloe said. "We'll go out." She had told MJ about Fig's doctor friend last night, and MJ, in her new role as chauffeur, had already volunteered to drive.

"Have fun," Kiki said, on her way down into a grand plié. "I'll be in rehearsal, but I think it's *high* time the two of you had fun!"

MJ had some trouble with the tango between clutch and gas, lurching, lurching, lurching up Hyde Street, but Chloe wasn't about to complain. She was feeling lucky MJ was here at all. And, anyway, if she closed her eyes, the hills were Kiki-ish fun, like inching to the top of a roller coaster, the last car of the ride. In the moment they'd crested a hill and the car seemed momentarily airborne, the aaahhhhhh before the drop, Chloe let out a little yip.

At a plateau, MJ pulled into a parking lot in the middle of the block, between the fancy Grace Cathedral and the fancier Fairmont Hotel. "I'll walk into the doctor's lobby for a second," MJ said. "In case he's a kook and you've got to get out of there."

The building was low and blah. As soon as MJ opened the double glass doors, though, Chloe could see this doctor's office was nicer and more iridescent than yesterday's place. It was like an airport, white and shiny.

Chloe lowered her chin and whispered, "Do you think they know why I'm here? Can you see an invisible scarlet *A*?" Chloe's hair had worked free of its clip and swooped over one eye.

"Who cares about *The Scarlet Letter*? For a book about lust, it was bo-*ring*."

The all-business receptionist handed Chloe forms and a perfectly sharpened pencil. Chloe liked forms, liked filling up blank ovals. She liked the SAT for this el-cheapo reason. She even liked the occupational quiz she took junior year, which showed she had an aptitude for flower arranging and also law.

While shading in the various bubbles, Chloe imagined she was somewhere else, in college or on a job interview, and that the answers meant something else, that she would ace the class or win the case, but, unfortunately, the questions were pretty pointed. Which of the following conditions best described her: Depressed? Anxious? Suicidal? Change in weight? Change in sleeping pattern? Jittery? Paranoid? Hopeless?

Chloe didn't have anything to shade in.

"If you're cool, I'm going to split." MJ rummaged around her leather bag until she extracted one of Kiki's many apartment keys. She pressed the baby-blue rabbit's-foot keychain into Chloe's hand. "Hold this. For luck. I'll meet you back at the car. I might check out that church."

"More praying?"

MJ shrugged. "For the hell of it."

Chloe wondered if the foot was genuine, removed from an authentic woodland creature.

"Dr. Reed is ready for you," a nurse with bangs said. "Just hand him those." She pointed at Chloe's forms and clicked her pen, off/on, off/on, off/on.

The inner office radiated with a silvery wallpaper. Light bounced from one wall to another, a sunshine tennis ball.

"Can I get you a croissant?" Dr. Reed asked. He stroked his walrus mustache. It was salty gray.

He opened a Lucite cabinet. With a pair of tongs, he placed a croissant on each of two lime-green plates.

To be polite, Chloe took a bite. The last thing her stomach needed was puffy pastry.

"Now, tell me what I can do for you. I know you're a buddy of Fig's."

"I'd like . . . well, I wouldn't like. I need an abortion," Chloe said.

"That would have been my guess. Let's take a look-see," said Dr. Reed, giving Chloe's forms a glance. "I notice you didn't circle any suicidal thoughts. You left that open. We are in this strange culture right now where you must convince me that you are unbalanced. Tell me. Are you feeling suicidal? California law allows abortion if it saves the mother's life. Think about it. Think about suicide."

"Sure." Inside her clogs, Chloe crossed her toes.

He nodded. "I don't want to coach you too much, I'm just saying it would speed things up if you mention suicide."

"You mean actually say it?"

He nodded again, more faintly.

"Oh, suicide," Chloe said. She had a knot in her throat.

"Okay. Now I can recommend a termination," Dr. Reed said. His tie was alive with wildflowers.

"Oh, phew. Thank you." Chloe fiddled with her notebook in her lap.

Dr. Reed laughed. "Phew it is. Now, I notice you are here on your own. I applaud that." He clapped his hands. "And it's not my place to intrude, but as you are a minor, I wonder if you've made arrangements for parental involvement."

"I will," Chloe said. She should, so that was technically true.

"Hmmm." Dr. Reed used both hands to smooth the walrus into submission. "What I hear you saying is you're having trouble asking for the emotional succor to get this done."

Was that what she'd said? "I guess."

"The committee needs the PND, the Parental Notification Document, before the procedure, so if you're not going to have a parent with you—"

"*Before?*" Chloe asked. "I thought it was *at*. And committee? The social worker at the Women's Way mentioned it in passing. But my research didn't say anything about a committee."

Chloe thumbed through her notebook, rumpling pages, anxious to scan every one. "No committee, no committee. See?" She held up a page of neat and annotated notes. "No committee."

"Hey, hey, I didn't mean to freak you out. It's the Committee of Sterilization and Abortion—and it's routine. They meet, as needed, at the hospital and grant permission la-di-da-di-dah. We don't have time to go into that today." He stood up.

"Oh." Chloe figured they were done. "What's your fee?"

"Ah, a freebie," he said. "Scratch that. Here's my fee."

"Fifteen dollars?" Chloe asked. Then she figured his office was much sleeker than the one yesterday. "Twenty?"

"Dr. Reed leaned closer. "My fee is that you acknowledge this might be harder for you than you think. Forget about the committee. Even if you're a very together type, who keeps a journal or a to-do list or whatever you've got there, this is tough stuff. Be prepared to be surprised." He wiggled his fingers—to symbolize surprise, Chloe guessed.

Chloe had been mindlessly rubbing the rabbit foot, but her thumb landed on an odd indentation. A toe pad, perhaps. Dr. Gladstone had told Chloe that, until recently, doctors tested for pregnancy by injecting a rabbit with a girl's pee; a few days later, they'd kill the rabbit and check its ovaries. Chloe started wondering if this particular baby-blue foot came from a pregnancy bunny, and she dropped the key onto Dr. Reed's empty desk.

He handed the foot back. "Not to worry. The abortion itself is a snap!" He tried to snap his fingers together, but he was one of those awkward snappers. His fingers whisked past each other, making no noise. "It's the other stuff you've got to watch out for."

"I'm fine." But Chloe couldn't take her eyes off his thumb, which she'd learned in biology was called the *digitus primus* and was controlled by eight muscles. When would *This* form thumbs?

Dr. Reed opened a slim desk drawer and took out his prescription pad. His name was printed across the top in small, neat letters. In the center of the pad, he scrawled a prescription. It was like he was writing an order for cough medicine or the Pill, but instead he was signing a permission slip, a hall pass for an abortion. Behind the prescription, he attached his business card with a small gold paperclip.

Chloe made an inside promise, the kind that was easy to break, that she would start the Virginia note. She didn't have to figure out why it was hard to do, she just had to do it.

"If you ever feel snowed under, give a ring," he said.

On the way out, Chloe flipped the rabbit's foot over, toe over heel, wondering why it was supposed to bring luck, anyway. It wasn't like it worked so well for the rabbit.

MJ was waiting by the car, rosary beads in hand.

"Did you go into the church?" Chloe asked.

"Yeah, it was Episcopal with stained-glass windows of, like, Robert Frost. But a cathedral is a cathedral. When in Rome . . ."

The knot was back in Chloe's throat. "I'm glad. I mean, if you're glad you went, then I am, too."

"I just lit a candle, that's all. How did it go in there? Better than last time?"

"Yeah, thank God. I got what I needed," Chloe said. Part of it, anyway.

Back at Kiki's place, Chloe went into a cleaning frenzy, washing the kitchen cabinets, which were thick with dust. She dunked her hands into soapy, piney suds and scrubbed. On the first pass, the grime just smudged, but eventually Chloe elbowed her way down to the original white wood.

MJ kept her company, flipping through a newspaper, running her finger down the pages, trying to find something interesting. "It's all war, war, and failed peace," she said with a sigh. She chucked the paper and turned her attention to the pantry. The shelves were stacked with pickled vegetables and bulk grains. On a canister of brown rice was a sticker: MAKE BROWN RICE, NOT WAR.

"Think there's a Twinkie?" MJ asked. "A Ho-Ho would be excellent. I'd even go for one of my mom's Jell-O molds." Mrs. Donnelly had a collection of Tupperware molds in various shapes.

Chloe stood up fast, thinking about lime Jell-O with pineapple, and Teddy, and reflexively she ran her tongue over her teeth, trying to remember when she'd last brushed.

As if reading Chloe's mind, MJ said, "I'm gonna meet up with Teddy's foxy roommate to bum around the city. Come with, if you want. We should keep you busy. What do you think flaxseed tastes like?" MJ asked, holding up a cookie.

"I'll stay and clean out Kiki's pantry, maybe alphabetize her spices."

MJ took a bite of the cookie and spit it out in the sink. "Yuck. What's your next step? For the thing, I mean."

"To write a note from Virginia."

"Big whoop, a note." MJ rolled her eyes a full revolution.

Chloe fingered her curls, inspecting the ends for splits. "I wish Virginia could appear, write the note, then disappear."

"I'm here, and now I'm going to disappear." MJ changed into a pucker shirt and took off.

From her duffel, Chloe took out her Flair felt-tips, a rainbow of colors under a plastic sleeve, and tried different Virginia-isms, not worrying about the handwriting for the moment, but trying to convey her mother on paper.

"I understand that my daughter, Chloe Switzer, intends to go through with the act of an abortion. I believe in her absolute right, as I believe in the right of all women, to make this decision.

"My only child, Chloe Switzer, has my permission to proceed with the abortion she has a state-given right to obtain.

"I have raised my daughter, Chloe Switzer, to be self-sufficient and, above all, not stupid, and yet, in this instance, she has failed. Therefore, after the mess she has created, I have no choice but to grant her wish for an abortion."

It reminded Chloe of Virginia dictating the proper way to write thank-you notes for Chloe's Bat Mitzvah. "Don't start a note with 'thank you for.' That's unoriginal," Virginia declared. "Come at things sideways."

Chloe kicked back on the futon, remembering how Virginia was into the feminist manifesto of the whole Bat Mitzvah, since it was almost always a boys-only ritual, especially at her temple in Phoenix, where she was only the second girl to do it.

Virginia was also into Chloe then—for taking the Bat Mitzvah on, for learning the trope, for looking righteous. For what seemed like weeks after the worship service, Virginia kissed Chloe's head or squeezed her shoulder. "I'm raining love for you," she'd said, and Chloe had wanted to hold on to that feeling. She'd wanted to be an ornamental cactus in their yard, drawing on wisps of odd showers during arid spells.

Chloe tried coming at it sideways. "My daughter, Chloe Switzer, has acted irresponsibly. Even so, she should be allowed to have an abortion at age seventeen."

It wasn't until she wrote her age that it hit Chloe's front consciousness that Virginia hadn't been much older than seventeen when she'd had Chloe. Virginia was twenty when Chloe was born, so she was nineteen, a number that still ended with a "teen," when she was a few weeks pregnant. Maybe Virginia had wanted to write such a note herself.

And maybe if she had, Chloe didn't want to know.

CAROB AND CABLE CARS

It was pretty late when the front door clicked open. Kiki stood bull's-eyed in the doorway wearing mind-blowing velvet hot pants.

"Oh, good. Here you are," she said. "Time for ice cream."

"Now? You just got home."

"Sure, now! I'm like an eight-year-old. No impulse control."

Chloe checked Snoopy. It was almost eleven.

"*C'mon,*" Kiki lobbied. "Who turns down ice cream?"

Arms interlocked, Chloe and Kiki walked up and up Broadway, past Columbus, past the girlie-show callers—*Come see titty history! Be liberated! Go topless! Whadda I see? 44DDD!*—to Hyde Street, where the cable car ran. The streets were more crowded than they were early in the day, with guys on stilts and zither players in swirly embroidered skirts. There was a whiff of sour wine or maybe BO.

Chloe missed the smell of Arizona desert, which was to say, the smell of nothing.

"Don't only tourists take the cable car?" Chloe asked.

"No, only tourists stay on long enough to pay," Kiki answered, jumping on the running board. She pulled Chloe up behind her and knocked on the top of her head for luck, like she used to do a million years ago.

Before Kiki had moved to San Francisco, she'd lived in Phoenix, too, seven houses away from Chloe, from what was then Chloe and Virginia, plus Chloe's dad and Blue, the peek-a-poo (a Pekinese-poodle mix). Kiki turned up almost every night for dinner with alfalfa sprouts or Japanese cucumbers, something exotic for the salad.

Once, for Virginia's birthday, Kiki came over with a grocery bag of baking ingredients. "Shhh!!" she whispered, thin finger to her lips. "I'm stoned!" She smelled like grass just after a rain. While the house was quiet, Kiki and Chloe baked sour cream cupcakes—sour cream was the secret. It kept the batter moist.

They were awesome cupcakes, especially the gooey frosting made with melted marshmallows. Chloe held a finger lick of frosting against the roof of her mouth, wanting it to stay there forever. Between the five of them—Virginia, Chloe, Dad, Kiki, dog—they ate all eighteen cupcakes.

Kiki split in the summer of 1968, the summer the Youngbloods sang *smile on your brother, everybody get together, try to loooove one another right now.* She called three days later and announced she was a flame and, poof, she was out and could only be relit in San Francisco. The rest of the family unknotted soon after. Dad went off to Oregon, needing a whole new climate to start over. Virginia went off to find herself, over and over again. Even Blue took off, burrowing under the fence to freedom one day while Chloe was at school.

❊   ❊   ❊

The cable car lurched, and Kiki hopped off in front of Swenson's with Chloe right behind.

It turned out the tiny shop had closed for the night. Kiki rapped on the glass door, and a girl with rainbow suspenders waved and opened up. Apparently, they knew each other from acting class.

Kiki placed the order—a double scoop of mint chocolate chip for Chloe and a double orange carob ripple for herself.

With a tiny paper napkin, Chloe wiped down the inside windowsill, and they perched in silence, licking their respective cones.

After a while Kiki asked, "So, what's shaking with you?"

Chloe held a chocolate chip against her teeth until it melted, making a note to double-brush that night. "Not a lot."

With her noncone hand, Kiki took Chloe's noncone hand and kissed it for some reason.

It was a surprising feeling, Chloe realized, to be kissed by a family member. As Kiki would say, it was a wow of a surprise.

"Because I have this sense," Kiki continued. "There's something different in your aura."

Chloe figured it was the usual Kiki flakiness. "Are you talking about the box you had me put my feelings into? I've been trying to keep the lid on that box. Maybe it needs to be wrapped in tin foil or something." Chloe caught sight of a box of sugar cones on Swenson's counter and wondered if someone who was here earlier had tried to transport her feelings—of loneliness or possibility or whatever—to some innocent cones.

"Hmmm," Kiki said. She looked right at Chloe.

"Because walking around with Teddy was weird," Chloe explained somewhat after the fact.

"I think that's less important."

Was it? Were they still talking about Teddy?

Kiki seemed to soak up the silence. She methodically licked her cone. After a long minute, she said, "Fig mentioned something about a *friend* needing to see a certain psychiatrist. I know a friend is never a friend. What's going on?"

Chloe leaned her head back against the glass. The window was cold and refreshing. She wanted it to be even colder, to make her numb. Her mind was spinning Spirograph shapes, intricate, complicated drawings, the little teeth of the plastic gears grinding away to reveal some great picture, some happy ending, just a few more revolutions away.

"I'm pregnant," Chloe said. "Almost four weeks. Or almost six if you count the way doctors count."

"Wow, a baby? That's heavy," Kiki said. She stretched her arm open and Chloe folded herself into Kiki's shoulder. Kiki rocked her gently, back and forth, forth and back.

Chloe wiggled free to chuck the rest of her cone into the trash.

"What about names?" Kiki asked. "I like Willow. There's this chick over on Fillmore—"

"That's not the plan," Chloe said. "The plan is—"

"Oh, I know, I'm just dreaming." Kiki motioned to her lap, but Chloe didn't want to roost. She sat facing her aunt instead. "You're going to free-choice it! You'll be all 'Get your laws off my body.' Am I right?"

"Sort of."

"I get it, I do. More ice cream!" Kiki went back to the counter to order another orange carob ripple.

"I need to lock up soon," the rainbow-suspendered girl said, handing the cone over. She'd already mopped the place twice.

"We're dealing with a family emergency," Kiki said. She eyed the tip jar—DIG US? THEN GIVE IT TO US!—and stuffed in a crumpled dollar bill.

Back at the windowsill, between licks, Kiki said, "I've heard if the cells are really small, you can trick yourself into a hiccupping fit and change your karma and—"

"Abortion!" Chloe interrupted. "I have a consultation for an abortion," she said in a lower voice. "Tomorrow."

Kiki put her hand on Chloe's cheek and left it there. "You know, this is good for you. A little fuck-up. It's not good for a person to be perfect. Perfection is boring."

Chloe didn't know what to do with her hands. She sat on them. "It's not legal in Arizona. But here, where you are, here it's all possible." She looked out the big window into the starless night. Somewhere downhill was the bay, but without seeing or hearing it, you could forget you were anywhere special.

"You don't need to obfuscate—ooh, Kiki uses a big word. Don't hide or keep secrets. Take that window you're looking through," Kiki said, following Chloe's eyes. "Sparrows smash into that window on a regular basis."

Whatever the hell that meant.

"Let's make sure you don't smash," Kiki said with an enigmatic smile.

By the time they left Swenson's around midnight, the cable car had stopped running. Chloe and Kiki started the long walk home. Except it turned out that taking the cable car was actually the slow way around.

"What does all this have to do with the boy we've put in the box?" Kiki asked, after a few blocks.

"Nothing. Nothing at all."

Kiki seemed to get it. "So you're in a fix with the *bad* kisser. Okay, I'm following. Let me help you in the now."

Chloe stepped back from the curb, waiting for the light to turn green. "In the now I'm getting an abortion. Well, in the now I'm pregnant."

Kiki looped her arm around Chloe's waist and gave her a kiss on the cheek. Kiki was in quite the kissy mood.

"You're the only one who knows the whole truth about everything," Chloe said. "I can't talk to MJ about Teddy—she'd kill me. I can't talk to Teddy about the abortion—he'd kill me. Or hate me." Chloe bit her lip.

Kiki flung her arms up, sharing her good idea with the night sky. "More sage may be required."

The fog was rolling in, hushing the sounds. Chloe felt like she was wearing earmuffs.

A few blocks later, Kiki said, "I'm going to take a *wiiiild* guess that you haven't told Virginia. I like being the one to know, but you've put me in a tight spot. She's my family, too."

They turned down Union Street, and Chloe listened to the sound of their feet slapping the sidewalk. She stopped in front of a cute restaurant named Rumpelstiltskin, checking out the menu taped in the window, wondering what would happen if she ate cheese fondue, which was listed right there under "starting appeasements." Would she be able to follow MJ's cheer and woo-hoo-hoo it up? Wouldn't it be nice if happiness could be ordered for $3.95 at a place with checkered curtains?

"Wait." Kiki stopped and spun around. "Don't you *need* Virginia?"

"Not Virginia herself, just her permission. I'm writing a note on her behalf," Chloe said.

"I dig your independence, but I want to go with you." Kiki twirled her hair around. Virginia had the same blond hair, although hers was short and shaglike. "I want to feed you ice chips or Greek yogurt."

What would be wrong with having a little emotional succor, as Fig's doctor friend would say?

"Maybe," Chloe said. "But what I really want is for this . . . experience . . . to stay in San Francisco."

"*Sin* Francisco," Kiki corrected her.

LET IT ROLL

"**W**atch out—here I come!" Kiki announced, loud enough to wake the stale morning air of the kitchen, where Chloe and MJ were contemplating breakfast.

Chloe turned from the table to see Kiki on roller skates, the wheels humming as they skimmed the wooden floor.

"I woke up inspired! You know what today is?" Kiki asked.

"I know. My come-and-go appointment," Chloe said.

MJ shot her a look.

"I told."

"Well, that," Kiki said. "But also New Year's Eve eve! When we wake up two days from now, it will be a whole new year, a clean slate." She seemed unsteady, even though all eight wheels were on the ground.

Chloe briefly wondered if she should lace up a pair of skates. Klutz that she was, she could fall and resolve *This* on her own.

As if reading her mind, MJ said, "We could rent skates and zoom down a few hills. Accidents happen."

Kiki swatted at the air, dismissing them. "Plus, plus, plus, it's almost the Nude Relay, and I have to think up my booth. The first year I did a kissing station. Last year I tried a dildo ring toss. This year I have to top myself."

"Want to top yourself? Go topless. Who doesn't love that?" Fig mused. He'd appeared over Kiki's shoulder.

The phone rang, and Kiki grabbed it.

"Yes, yes, we're fine, Virginia. Quiet. Reading poetry," Kiki said, a wink Chloe's way. "Miss Chloe is here. Happy almost New Year to you."

Kiki skated the receiver over.

"Good morning, Virginia," Chloe said.

"What did you do yesterday?" Virginia asked, sounding far away.

"We had ice cream. How about you?" Silently, she added, *Please don't tell me about Stan.*

"Don't overdo the sugar. It makes you break out. I do hope that you and MJ take advantage of the culture the city has to offer. I called over to the DeYoung Museum."

Chloe could imagine Virginia peering over her reading glasses at her carefully written notes.

"They have a traveling exhibit of African masks that sounds worth taking in. You don't need my permission to do something good for you, you know?"

"Uh, what?" Chloe was weirded out that Virginia was talking about permission. It was as if her long-latent mother sense was coming out of hibernation.

"Go forward and see the African masks," Virginia repeated.

"Okay," Chloe said distractedly. She pictured Virginia's handwriting on permission slips, the *V* exaggerated like a giant check mark.

Her stomach burbled. "I've got to run, Virginia." Chloe returned the receiver to its home on the wall, then went to the bathroom for her morning vomit deposits.

"Now, where was I?" Kiki said, when Chloe rejoined the kitchen. Kiki spun around, her arms lifted in a touchdown pose. "Right! My booth. I'm thinking playful. I'm thinking . . . erotic balloon animals."

MJ vigorously whisked a bowl of pancake batter. "Chloe twisted balloons at my sister's birthday party. Not erotic ones, though."

"Unless you count the extra appendage for the kangaroo," Chloe added.

MJ snorted. "Where's the griddle, Kiki? I'm making my famous pancakes before Chloe's appointment."

"I wasn't half bad at it. The balloons, I mean," Chloe said. After three days of waiting, or twenty-six, depending on how she counted (or thirty-seven if she was using little Annie's math), her appointment with the actual doctor who had the power and the permission to end *This* had arrived. It was like a holiday circled on the calendar, except there was no "happy" or "merry."

"A griddle?" Kiki's head snapped around. "God, how suburban. Try this." She used the rubber toe stop on the skate and leaned into a low cabinet. Her head and shoulders disappeared. After a few clattering moments, she emerged, wok in hand.

"Hell, why not?" MJ laughed.

"So how exactly did you do the animals? Is there a lot of artistry involved?" Kiki asked, pointing a heavy skate at Chloe. "Sit."

Chloe pulled the step stool up to the counter. "There weren't directions. I just twisted until it looked like something."

"Coffee?" Fig asked.

Kiki shook her head. "Don't interrupt. I have only today and tomorrow to get a booth together. I need all hands on deck." Her serious tone was at odds with the absurdity of her feat.

"We don't need to, uh, relay, right?" MJ asked.

"Righto," Fig said. "Gawkers are welcome, right, your *high*-ness." Behind MJ's back he pantomimed taking a few tokes. "The city doesn't endorse the relay, but they don't stop us either. They let it slide!" Fig said, a gleam in his eye as he walked under the sharp overhead light toward the sink. He put a filter in the glass coffeepot shaped like a beaker.

MJ slipped the spatula down the slope of the wok and with a quick wrist flick launched the buckwheat pancake up and out of the wok. Fig ducked. The pancake splatted on a plate.

"Hungry?" she asked.

"No thanks," he said. "I prefer wheat germ."

MJ handed Chloe a plate with three imperfect pancakes. Kiki didn't have anything as conventional as syrup. The pancakes had a slight after-taste of kung pao sauce from the wok, but they were still pretty great.

"This is the best breakfast I've had in ages," Chloe said.

Kiki stopped making figure eights. "Are you trying to knock our Virginia? Please don't criticize your mother."

"Virginia doesn't cook anymore," Chloe said in midbite.

"She's too liberated," MJ agreed.

"That's not cool, Clo. Virginia fed you well," Kiki said. "She would have a salad, and you would have the lamb chop. Where do you think I learned to cook? At the elbow of Virginia. She might not dig tempeh or tahini, or the stuffed peppers and beef stroganoff or whatever Betty Crocker fare is served up at the Donnelly house, no offense, MJ—"

MJ was washing the batter bowl. "It's okay. We do have a lot of casseroles."

Kiki closed her eyes, as if trying to conjure up those afternoons in the kitchen. "To Virginia it's not the ingredients but the *substance*. Where did you cry over Bobby Kennedy lying in a pool of nearly black blood? Where did you learn an abortion was even something to fight for? Over a meal at that oval kitchen table."

Chloe thought Kiki's recollection was half right. There was no image of Virginia picking through a salad. Chloe could only picture her at the stove, her back to the table, perhaps surreptitiously gnawing a bone. But the talk, that much was true.

After showering, Chloe put on immaculate white underwear from a fresh plastic bag, and a jeans skirt she'd made from an old pair of Levi's the week she'd learned about *This*. She'd split the seams of the crotch and legs and added a patch of calico across the front and butt to give herself growing room, although she hadn't really grown. Now the seam was fraying a fraction of an inch at a time.

Chloe checked her bag: Dr. Reed's paperwork, her notebook with the doctor's address, and, in the hidden compartment, her cash.

"Ready to boogie?" Kiki asked. She'd changed into a turquoise minidress with a giant zipper down the front. Chloe guessed it could pass for grown-up in San Francisco.

The air felt misty as they buckled up in the Lady Bug for the short ride to the come-and-go part of the hospital, MJ behind the wheel, in her new chauffeur role, Chloe in the passenger seat, and Kiki flaked out in the back. By the time they hit Van Ness, Kiki had slipped into a nap, snoring lightly.

As MJ made the final turn, Chloe could see a cluster of people crowded together near the side entrance to the hospital. She thought it might be a group of antiwar protesters, shaking placards like a twenty-armed octopus.

The closer MJ drove to the parking lot, the clearer the picture. These weren't antiwar/antidraft/pro–Indian rights/pro-feminism marchers. These were antiabortion protesters, and they were here protesting people like her.

MJ flipped up the radio, trying to drown out the chants.

"What's abortion? Wrong! What's abortion? Wrong!" It wasn't even a good cheer.

Moby Grape was on the radio. It was the chorus of that song "The Place and the Time," the one where *nothingggg, nothingggg* is repeated a million times.

"Holy shit," MJ said. She flicked on the turn signal.

Chloe hoped that once MJ pulled into the lot, the placards and their holders would stay on the sidewalk, but it was a traveling circus.

As soon as MJ edged between the painted lines of a parking spot, a grandmother type with a large wooden cross stood in front of the car, centering herself.

Before Chloe could open the passenger door, two women in dreary double-knit dresses were at her window, wagging pamphlets.

"Can I do a U-ie?" MJ asked, looking out the rear window. "Can I haul ass out of here? I'll park a few blocks away."

A woman with gray curls hurled herself against the back wind-shield. MJ and Chloe screamed.

"Killer!" the protester yelled, her face streaked with something that looked sort of like blood. "Your baby has a heartbeat. Even if you can't hear it, it's there. Lub, dub. Lub, dub."

The commotion woke Kiki. "Why so loud?" And then, as she took in the scene, she sat up. "How dare they!"

"Please, please, don't freak out," Chloe said, her chest registering smidges of panic. "MJ doesn't even want to be here. Let's walk in without a big . . . without a big ruckus."

"Oh, NO." Kiki pushed Chloe's seat forward and got out of the car.

Chloe got out too, running her tongue nervously along her teeth.

Kiki windmilled her arms in giant circles, scaring people back. "Get your signs off her body." Kiki drew Chloe close. "What else do you oppose? Drinking and driving? That kills! Why don't you march outside a liquor store? Make a fucking poster: Scotch slaughters!"

Inside the Bug, Chloe could see MJ's head on the steering wheel.

A woman with a collaged photo of a fetus in a garbage can pointed at Kiki. "*Sheeee* is a daughter of Satan. *Sheeee* is giving her child a deathday instead of a birthday."

Kiki could really yell. "Don't hurl hateful things! What is wrong with you?" she asked the dreary duo. "What you're doing here, it can't be legal."

"Kiki, it *is* legal," Chloe said, trying to be heard above the fray. She knew that wasn't what most people would be thinking about in that moment, but it seemed hugely important to get the law right. It was *all* legal: the abortion—at least here—and the free speech. If the activists had been protesting the war (Hell, No, We Won't Go) Kiki would have joined them.

Someone paraded a poster in front of the Lady Bug—DON'T KILL YOUR BABY in big bubble letters.

MJ backed up fast, letting the protesters scamper out of her way.

Another car pulled into the lot, and the signs reconfigured themselves, like one of those chaotic blobs in a lava lamp, separating then clumping together around the new car.

"I'll pray for you," one of the older protesters said to Chloe.

"Don't you dare," Kiki said within spitting distance of his eye.

"I'll pray for myself!" Chloe said. She took Kiki's hand and hotfooted it into the building, where the chaos gave way to silence.

MELLOW MUSHROOM

It looked like a regular doctor's office. No blood, no scrubs, no gurneys. Chloe checked out her seatmates in the waiting room: two girls in matching Grateful Dead T-shirts; a woman with elegant posture and cornrows; a small brunette with a smaller, screaming child; and a mother-aged woman in a suede vest.

Chloe was the last one called to the back by a nurse with pixie hair. Kiki followed. The exam room was wallpapered in a granny floral, heavy on the pink, as if to make a girl think she was in a country inn.

There was no spare chair, so Kiki sat cross-legged on the doctor's scale on the floor, centering her ass on the little platform with a satisfied humph.

"I'm just here for a consolation," Chloe said, trying to take control of the appointment.

Kiki laughed from the scale. "You don't mean *consolation*. Like consolation prize."

"Con-sul-TA-tion," Chloe corrected herself.

"I know." The nurse left and shut the door behind her.

"Did those morons get to you out there?" Kiki asked Chloe. "If they did, we'll come back another time when you're stronger. For today, our asses can be grasses."

"I'm fine," Chloe said, dipping her chin down.

"Good! Good for you." Kiki exhaled. "Then let's do what I know how to do: Change the subject! Will you help with my booth? You don't have to do the nudie if you don't want to. Girl's choice."

"I'll choose no." The very last thing Chloe wanted to do was take off her clothes in front of anyone right now.

"You can always change your mind once we're there. It's wonderful to feel the air against your skin. So much of the time we are covering ourselves, who we really are to one another. It's easier to be true and honest when you're not hiding behind clothes. I say nude it up," Kiki said.

"I know you're trying," Chloe said. "But please. Shh."

Kiki giggled. "Right, sssssshhhh. I'm not even high anymore." She stood and faced the scale. It was a classic doctor's model, with fifty-pound increments on the bottom and a little sliding bar on the top for each quarter pound. Kiki slid the bottom lever to 100 then down to 50.

"Shit," she said softly when the arrow settled at 91. "When I'm under a hundred, I get this absurdly convex chest."

Chloe looked down at her own, not-convex chest.

Kiki stepped off the scale and said, "Jump on. Let's see what the little pea you're carting around has done to your poundage."

"I'm trying not to think about the pea, Keeks. If you could be . . ."

Chloe thought of saying *normal*, but instead chose *quiet*. "If you could be quiet, I would deeply appreciate it."

Chloe wondered if there was a scale that could weigh individual parts instead of a whole. What would her head weigh? Her long hair, wet then dry? Her breasts? Or *This*?

"Knock, knock, I'm Liberty," a different nurse said, opening the door without waiting for a response. She reached out to shake Chloe's hand, and Chloe noticed her nails were bitten all the way down. She was grateful to have a nurse with flaws.

"I'm Chloe. And this is Kiki," Chloe said, gesturing to the scale.

Kiki gave a little wave.

Whoa. Chloe had been so busy checking out Liberty's nails that she had missed the bigger picture. Liberty was pregnant; a perfect bump protruded from her belly.

"My job is to help you understand your options and then, if you choose to go forward, to prepare you before you see Dr. Thain on"— she looked at the chart—"January third."

Chloe couldn't make her eyes move from the nurse's stomach.

"You all right there, Clo?" Kiki asked.

Chloe nodded, but her shoulders said otherwise. They did a little shimmy.

Liberty took Chloe's medical history—allergies, medications, vaccinations, hospitalizations—and did a quick workup, checking Chloe's blood pressure, ears, throat, nose, temperature.

"Do you have the doctor's prescription for the procedure?" Liberty's eyes were smiling, not mocking.

Chloe ironed the slip with her fingers, wanting it to be perfectly smooth, not crazy looking.

"Now"—Liberty sat on the end of the exam table with a small grunt—"I've got to ask you a series of questions written by a bunch of men designed for the express purpose of flipping you out."

Chloe thought that Liberty would make a fun mom.

"I'm obligated to tell you that we have phone numbers for maternity homes and adoption referral services. You could still choose to have the child."

Chloe pressed her lips together and shook her head.

"Are you interested in investigating adoption?"

"Oh, God, I couldn't." Chloe flashed on protesters praying for her and on Liberty's ripe belly and wished she'd phrased it differently. "I just know. I couldn't."

"Is this your decision? Is anyone urging you to do something you don't want to do?" Liberty had probably gone to training sessions to learn to take all judgment out of her voice.

"It's a hundred percent my decision." Saying that made Chloe feel better, stronger. "Two hundred percent."

Kiki was conspicuously silent during this part of the conversation. Chloe worried Kiki was some other percentage sure—fifty or twenty or ten.

With her bitten-off nails, Liberty paperclipped the prescription to the outside of a manila file folder with Chloe's name typewritten on a yellow label.

"Here's what will happen," Liberty said. "We'll prep you, dilate the cervix, and insert a small tube. That attaches to a pump. Then we pump the matter into a bottle." She slowly gestured, in and out, with her hands, and Chloe couldn't get the image of an accordion out of her mind. "We'll give you pain medication. The procedure takes five minutes, but you'll be here a few hours—an hour before, two hours after. Okay?"

Chloe instinctively stroked her belly. She remembered the psychiatrist snapping his fingers, or trying to. The procedure didn't sound like such a snap after all. And that, for some reason, made her feel better.

Liberty eased herself off the exam table. "Do you have questions for me?"

From her bag, Chloe took out her notebook. In the front were her pretty pages—sketches of various tops she loved, favorite quotes written in bubble letters. In the back were all her research notes. In the middle, between the rhythm of the ruled lines, were her real questions.

"Will I see anything? I don't want to, I mean."

"No." Liberty nibbled a hangnail on her thumb.

"Will I be awake?"

"You'll have a choice—knocked out a lot or a little."

"Will there be a lot of blood?" The morning's kung pao–laced pancakes threatened to force their way back up Chloe's throat.

Liberty lowered her thumb to check her handiwork. "Like a period. The cell cluster is less than an inch at this point."

Chloe squinted at her thumb and forefinger, estimating an inch.

"You know, Clo, you've been very mellow mushroom about all this," Kiki said. "All your questions have been about your body. What about your head? What's going on in your head?"

"Will I regret it?" Chloe blurted out, even though she hadn't written that one down. It was the same question MJ had asked the day before in the park with the red-bereted baby.

"Sorry, but you know I can't answer that," Liberty said.

Chloe thought she saw the nurse's jaw clench slightly.

"Now, last thing, for your mom." Liberty handed Kiki a few forms.

Kiki cocked her head and started to say, "I'm—"

"Ready!" Chloe finished. She realized the nurse couldn't possibly think the beautiful twenty-eight-year-old in a turquoise minidress was her mother, but if she were going to solve the problem for her, Chloe would play along.

"Will you be there for the procedure, Mrs. Switzer? I can make a note of that in the file." Liberty's pen hovered over the form.

"I hope so, Mom," Chloe said, wishing she'd been unchicken enough to ask Kiki outright before.

Kiki looked neither surprised nor offended. "If I'm not able to be here, what then?"

"Then we'll need a PND, a note giving your minor child your permission to end the pregnancy. Chloe can bring it to the procedure, if necessary, although we like to have it beforehand, Mrs. Switzer."

"I go by *Ms.*," Kiki said.

And Chloe was reminded how easy it was to answer a question with both the truth and a lie.

"Oops, *last*, last thing," Liberty said, turning to Chloe. "What are you doing about birth control?"

Chloe felt her cheeks flash and flush. "Nothing. I mean, not now."

"Ah, then, help yourself." The nurse slid a drawer open beneath the scrub sink. It was filled to the brim with packets of condoms. She held up a ribbon of three condoms before leaving to double-check the schedule.

"Are we thinking the same thing?" Kiki asked, tapping her temple.

"About Virginia?"

Kiki scrunched her nose. "No. What do condoms remind you of? Starts with a *ball* and ends with an *oon*?"

"Oh, let's not," Chloe said, as Kiki pocketed a ribbon of condoms. "It feels funny, Kiki. Can't we just get them somewhere else?"

"She said 'help yourself.' We're just following directions."

A handful at a time, Kiki tossed the little foil packets, like so many after-dinner mints, into Chloe's bag. Ten, twenty, forty, eighty.

"All set," Liberty said, walking back into the room without a knock, knock. Chloe zipped her bag up. "Dr. Thain will see you in four days. The committee meets an hour before the procedure, but I don't see any issues getting in the way of your approval. Gumball for the road?" she offered, reaching into her pocket.

"Thanks," Chloe said, taking a purple one, even though she thought she'd taken plenty already.

Biting into the sour-grape gum brought Chloe back to the Saturday she and Shep got together-together. Chloe had been perfecting her bubble-blowing ability in the early evening outside the Corner Store. It took a good five minutes to reach blowing consistency. People rushed it. She liked to grind down every sharp fragment. Bubbles were such fragile beings. After endless tries, she'd blown a perfect globe. She could see the gossamer top of it when she'd peered down her nose.

"Sexy, sexy," Shep said. He'd rounded the corner in Levi's and a peach alligator shirt. He had, like, twenty alligator shirts. "You could just blow me instead."

Pop. "Don't you wish," Chloe said, hoping there wasn't gum debris on her nose.

"You know, I do. I do wish," he said.

Chloe worked the gum over, trying to blow another bubble, but no such luck.

"C'mon, what else are you doing? We could have fun together." Shep plucked what must have been a speck of gum off her lip. His bangs were sticking up, and it made his hair less intimidating.

The thought of something—and someone—so uncomplicated seemed sort of great. And his hair was sort of great, and he had a flirty, smirky smile that worked for her, too.

They'd climbed into Shep's car, and he'd shifted, without stalling out, to her glass house in the hills. She'd actually learned to drive stick with Shep in Driver's Ed. They were seated next to each other by fluke of alphabet (Chloe Switzer, Shep Tansey). Once, when Chloe had stalled out, Shep had tucked her hair behind her ear and whispered, "Go, let it all go." It had seemed like an excellent mantra, and she'd had a dumb crush on him and his cute hair since then.

Virginia was at an equal-rights rally that afternoon. Chloe'd opened the front door and caught a glimpse of herself in the mirrored squares in the foyer. The mirrors were supposed to give the house added sparkle, as if that was something a piece of glass could be trusted to do.

Shep had looped his arm around Chloe's waist, and they'd made out standing up, against the mirror. Chloe had twisted into him, Levi's to Levi's. She'd pressed and held. He was her isometric exercise.

From somewhere deep inside her head came a buzz, like a TV that took a few seconds to come to life after you turned it on. That's how it had felt to be with Shep—electric, but delayed and distant.

She might pretend otherwise now, but the isometrics and the

making out had felt pretty nice. Thoughts of Teddy and Coppertone and tan lines had flickered in, but Chloe had blinked them away. And for a second, she'd thought it was weird that neither she nor Shep said anything at all, but she'd listened to the sigh of the pillows. And because his hands felt good, and because who knew what Teddy was doing anyway, she had let it all go.

The protesters had thinned out. Only the older marchers remained. MJ was waiting around the corner and down the block in the car, rosary beads coiled on her lap. Chloe and Kiki got into their same seats.

"Was it as intense inside as it was outside?" MJ asked, starting the car and pulling out into the street.

"No," Chloe said. In the rearview mirror, she tried to catch Kiki's eye to see if she'd agree, to see, she guessed, if Kiki was up to being Virginia, but Kiki's eyes were shut tight.

"But . . . ," MJ prompted.

"It was still hard," Chloe said.

With her pointer finger, Chloe practiced Virginia's signature in the dust of the dashboard, trying to capture the forceful way Virginia leaned into her *V*. It brought back a dumb memory of eighth grade and the way Chloe used to write *Ms. Curt Davinroy* or *Chloe Davinroy* or *Curt loves Chloe* over and over in her spiral notebook. But it wasn't the same. That was about trying on a new life. *This* was about trying to write yourself out of the life you were in.

WATERBED WAVES

Chloe and MJ woke up with zero plans on the morning of New Year's Eve. It was the first day since they'd crossed the Golden Gate that Chloe didn't have an abortion to-do *to do*.

The one and only thing on the agenda was to help Kiki set up the condom booth at the Nude Relay, but they didn't have to leave for the park until seven that night. Until then, the day was their oyster, but since they were in San Francisco, it was their Dungeness crab.

"Oh good, we can get more of my namesake, my Maryjane," MJ said early in the morning.

"If you want." Chloe figured she owed her that and more.

But then MJ never brought it up again, and Chloe had the feeling some of the oomph had gone out of MJ's big bad radical plans for herself.

For hours they did nothing but sit, still in pajamas, and listen to Kiki's records. It was a mini Tower Records right there on the window seat, and they cued up one revelation after another. The Velvet Underground song "Rock and Roll" was the new anthem of their trip.

As soon as the song ended, Chloe picked the needle up and started the track again. She needed to hear the line *And baby, it was all alriiiiighttt* over and over. By the twentieth time, she'd pretty much mastered where to drop the needle without jumping the groove.

After an afternoon of nothing, Kiki came out of the bedroom looking fresh and young. Her hair was pulled back into a ponytail, and she'd changed into a white blouse and a flowery skirt. "I've been thinking we should gather in a sharing circle. There is some heavy stuff going on."

Before Chloe could object, Kiki took her by one hand and MJ by the other and lowered them to the dusty floor. "Who wants to share?"

Silence.

"I'll go first, then," Kiki offered. She fluttered her eyes closed. "Here's what I want to share. I'm feeling sad. I'm feeling sad that Chloe, who I love on a soul-to-soul level, has to go through such pain. Chloe, you next," Kiki said. "Use an 'I' statement. 'I feel . . .'"

"I feel . . . ," Chloe started. What? What did she feel? "I feel confused. Not about what to do but about . . . I don't know."

"That's a start. We'll go around again, so start thinking about what you're feeling for your next turn. MJ, you go."

"I feel . . . confused, too."

"Have your own feelings," Kiki said.

"Okay, I'm not that confused." MJ paused. "I'm worried."

"I acknowledge that," Kiki said. In a rush of words she added, "I feel kind of freaked out by having to be responsible for Chloe, my only sister's only child." She faced Chloe and put her hands on Chloe's shoulders. Their eyes were inches apart.

"I'm scared," Chloe said, concentrating on Kiki's astonishing lack of pores. "Of what will happen to me three days from now and then later."

MJ moved to the window seat. "I'm—still—worried. I've been praying. Don't laugh, Chloe."

"I'm not," Chloe said, her voice thick in her throat.

"I don't know what else to *do*," MJ said. "I tried saying the novena every hour for eight hours, but I'd keep forgetting a few hours in and end up having to start all over again. We're running out of time! And there are still, like, ten thousand saints I don't even know. Finally, I just decided to pray to Saint Jude, the patron saint of lost causes."

"It's okay," Chloe said, sitting next to MJ. In her head she added, *I'm OK—You're OK*.

"Wow, heavy. Heavy-osity," Kiki said.

MJ grabbed Chloe's hair, just the ends. "I don't want you to do it."

Chloe's eyes filled.

"Oh, girls," Kiki interjected. "I could be worried too, but we can always worry later. Now? Now it's time to get happy, hyper, happy, hyper, hayper, no hyp, oh, whatever. It's the Nude Relay!"

❊   ❊   ❊

It was funny that talk of taking clothes *off* led to trying clothes *on*. Kiki's closet was big, and it was a mess. Chloe started hanging stuff up, plucking skirts off the floor and arranging them by length: the minis together, then the middies, then the maxis. She turned all the hangers so they were facing the same direction on the closet rod.

"You two try on anything you want," Kiki said. "I'm getting some sage."

MJ put on a thin shirt with delicate embroidery and tied the shirt-tails at her waist, a perfect triangle of stomach showing.

Chloe considered following Kiki into the kitchen and getting another box from the oven, one big enough to contain her feelings about *This*. But it was so much work even to find those feelings that she lay down on Kiki's waterbed and let the water buoy her.

The smell of burnt sage, that nasty not-really-weed aroma, wafted into the bedroom before Kiki. "I am happy to announce," she said from the doorway, "that calls have been made, and the karma for the evening has been changed."

"What the hell does that mean?" MJ asked, fluffing up her hair.

"That means that great things should happen on New Year's Eve." Kiki dramatically blew out the sage. "And that's why Teddy and some of his Berkeley boys will meet us at the condom stand. The more twisters the better."

"Oh, yeah, I dig that!" MJ said.

"Kiki!" Chloe yelled, trying to prop herself up on her elbows amid the waves.

"Don't get up," Kiki said. "Relax. *Re-lax*. You know, a San Francisco

State student invented the waterbed. First he tried one filled with Jell-O."

"KIKI!" Chloe flopped back down, feeling like she was swimming in Jell-O, trying to get to the solid ground of her brain.

And solid ground, or lack of it, made her think of earthquakes, which were a dime-bag a dozen here. On her own personal Richter scale, feeling something for Teddy was a 6.0, while betraying MJ with Teddy was a 7.0. Worrying about whether Kiki would pretend to be Virginia was a 7.0, while having to forge a note from Virginia herself was, for some weird reason, an 8.0.

MJ went to shave her legs in the sink.

"Just see how you feel about him," Kiki whispered to Chloe, when they were alone. "See if you want to kiss him. One kiss! Leave all the sadness in 1971. Enter the New Year fresh. Fresh as a daisy."

Chloe had an inspired thought.

Maybe it wasn't *either/or*, but *and*.

"Copacetic?" Kiki asked.

As Chloe was getting dressed, Kiki came up behind her, paintbrush in hand.

In the spirit of practicing what she preached, Chloe let Kiki lead her to the mirror. Kiki licked a fine-pointed paintbrush, swirled it into a pot of white eye shadow, and dabbed small strokes on Chloe's cheeks. Kiki stood back, then dipped the brush into sapphire shadow and added two dots.

"Fig's out front in some creepy station wagon," MJ announced, hanging out the window.

"Now you look happy," Kiki said. Chloe had two tiny perfect

daisies with white petals and blue centers, almost like tears falling down her cheek.

She didn't quite look like herself—and maybe that was just the way to see Teddy. Maybe seeing Teddy with daisies on her cheeks and music in the air wouldn't set off her personal Richter scale. Or maybe it would, and maybe a little tremor wouldn't kill her.

CONDOM KANGAROO

"What took you so long?" Fig asked, beating the hood of the wood-paneled station wagon like a bongo.

"Threads. We had to play dress-up," Kiki said, giving him a kiss on the neck.

"Who cares what you wear to a Nude Relay?" he asked.

"Me!" MJ said. "If everyone else is naked, what I'm in stands out."

Chloe had on her denim skirt, which had unraveled only slightly more, and a top from Kiki's closet, billowy and paisley.

Fig and Kiki loaded up the condom-stand provisions and a laundry basket of underwear for Kiki's modern-theater performance, and they took off.

The lot at the Clown Alley, home of the best burger with avocado according to the sign, was full. People were spilling out of cars, speakers blaring, yahooing it up. Fig jerked the wagon into reverse and pulled around to the back of the building, alongside a Dumpster.

Chloe opened the passenger-side door and nearly keeled over from the smell of rotten pickles.

When Fig got out and stretched his arms, a sliver of his hairy stomach caught air. MJ emerged from the back seat with Kiki.

"What's up with your hair?" MJ grabbed Chloe's elbow and steered her to an empty spot at the edge of the lot, where the pavement stopped and the trees suddenly began, a place like Phoenix, which had alien palm trees planted in perfect rows, even though there was very little water.

"Lose these," MJ said, tugging on Chloe's braids.

Chloe had French-braided her hair in the car, her fingers flying, wanting to get it out of the way.

"You look twelve. And here." MJ handed her an unlit smoke. "You'll look older if you hold it." MJ was used to bossing her sisters, but she was probably right.

Chloe gave her half of what she wanted. She took the Marlboro but kept the braids.

"Good," MJ said.

Kiki opened the lift gate and unloaded a card table with a fake wood top, four folding chairs, and a plastic bag filled with the freebie condoms. She raked her hands through her blond hair, wild with anticipation. She wore a colorful Mexican tunic. The bright birds of paradise made her skin look washed out by contrast. "Everybody grab something. We'll set up by the finish line."

They traipsed a few blocks, MJ pulling up the rear. When Kiki stopped on Stanyan Street, near the Kezar entrance, Fig unfolded the table and chairs and asked, "Can a condom even be twisted? Shouldn't it be stronger than that?"

"Don't be a glass half empty! Chloe's done it," Kiki said.

"With *balloons*," Chloe said, although she knew it was too late to matter.

Kiki jabbed her hand into the bag and pinched out a foil-packed condom. She opened it and put the coiled rubber to her lips. With one big blow, she inflated the condom into an oval orb. Kiki twisted it into a knot. "See?"

Fig uncoiled one, too. He blew into it and spiraled the end around. "What do you think?"

"A flamingo? Maybe a kangaroo!" Kiki said. "Girls, you try."

The smell—half rubber, half dentist's office—brought Chloe back to her condom encounter with Shep, which dominoed into a memory of Virginia demonstrating the proper roll-down technique on a firm banana, in her early libber days.

Kiki set up a bong for donations and fanned the condom packages across the table. She pulled her hair into pigtails and coiled each side into a bun. It looked like skeins of yarn were attached to her ears.

Most people were still clothed, Chloe noticed. She relaxed and pulled up a chair.

MJ had bled into the crowd, but a few minutes later she surfaced with a bottle of beer, plus Teddy and the Berkeley boys. After quick introductions—Mark and Matt or Mike and Matt or Mark and Mike—MJ disappeared with one of the guys.

"Welcome to the adventure!" Kiki said to Teddy. "Pull up a chair and twist!"

"Hi," Chloe said.

Teddy walked behind Chloe. He leaned down and said, "I didn't know which girl was going to show up—the Chloe I knew from the summer or the hot-and-cold Chloe."

His breath was gentle on Chloe's ear.

"Want to help?" Chloe asked, thinking she just wouldn't answer his question. It wasn't really a question anyway.

"Hey, now that you've got company, it's time I split," Kiki said. To Chloe she whispered, "It won't change anything if you have a good time tonight, so why not, right?"

Kiki disappeared into the crowd, basket on her head, like an exotic woman from one of those *National Geographic* photo spreads, except instead of toting water, she was carrying lingerie.

Teddy sat down and pushed up the sleeves of an unfamiliar green sweater. Did he get it for Christmas? Chloe wondered, and then she wondered what she would have given him if they were still together, and if it would have been green. He bullshitted with customers while Chloe made abstract poodles or monkeys or hearts. The more baked the customers were, the more they appreciated Chloe's nonfigurative artistry.

It was getting dark, and people who stopped by the table wore less and less clothing.

"What's this?" a girl asked Chloe, holding a pair of condoms looped into giant ears.

"An elephant," Chloe said.

The girl squinted, her dark nipples poking through the holes of her crocheted vest. "Oh, I was thinking mouse."

"That works too."

A couple gave Chloe a five-dollar tip for three condoms "as is—in the packet, please." After that, Teddy said, "Let's check out the race."

Chloe pocketed Kiki's cash, fifty-two dollars, for safekeeping but left the condoms out, figuring if people needed a condom that badly, they could help themselves. She and Teddy followed a stream of people toward the center of the park, walking next to each other but also apart.

The race was supposed to start in about an hour. It was hard to tell how many people were there. A thousand or two thousand or five thousand.

As they neared the band-shell stage, a bearded guy in a Hawaiian shirt tapped the microphone.

"Testing . . . one, two, reef . . ." That got a laugh.

Teddy nodded to the beat of a distant steel drum.

A very pale girl with beautiful red hair pulled off her turtleneck and twirled to face the crowd. "Ahhhh-whoa-o. I'm Jane-o!" Her freckled boobs were front and center. Chloe couldn't find a place to put her eyes, although she noticed Teddy could and did.

"Happy New Year and salutations! It's the third annual Nude Relay," the bearded guy said. "We started three years ago, in sixty-nine. The sexual position also known as *soixante-neuf*. Anyone care to demonstrate?"

"This is wild," said Teddy.

Chloe's cheeks turned hot, and she was grateful for the dark.

A bare-chested guy in low-slung jeans passed around a plastic pumpkin filled with leftover Halloween candy. "Trick or treat!" he said.

"What were you for Halloween?" Chloe yelled toward Teddy.

"Myself."

"I was a pirate." Chloe's head filled with images of kids in shiny costumes. She knew she was just incubating cells, but she wondered if they were the type of cells that would, if given the chance, like to dress up for Halloween. Something must be wrong-wired in her head. When she thought about Teddy, *This* intruded. And when she thought about *This*, there was Teddy. She exhaled even though she hadn't known she'd been holding her breath.

"Arrgh!" Teddy said, throwing his arm over her shoulder for a second.

Chloe took a Snickers bar and then wondered if it was laced with something. She passed it on to an outstretched hand, one of the dozens bending and swooning around her little patch of grass.

"A-lo-*ha!*" the emcee said as a couple, undressed except for their Birkenstocks, took the stage. "Now, why don't you orient yourself," he said to the woman, steering her by the shoulders, "such that your mouth is near . . . yes, there. And you, sir, you be the yang to her yin."

Chloe quickly spun around so her back was to the stage. "I went to the monthly antiwar protest at the statehouse. There were streakers there. Well, just one, but still, it's not like this is my first time."

Teddy smiled. "You're funny when you're nervous."

So many things were going on. A guy with gray hair plucked away on the mandolin, while a group of girls, maybe from Mills College, were doing the grapevine, snaking in and around a bunch of guys in drag hooting it up in prairie skirts. The whole night, broadcast over the crackling microphone, felt alive-live-live. Chloe had no idea where Kiki and Fig had set up their performance.

The runners gathered to the left of the stage. Oddly, given *This*, Chloe had never seen a guy naked. Parts of Teddy, yes. Parts of Shep, yes. But not a whole person flapping in the breeze. She looked down, trying to zero in on individual blades of grass.

"Tempted?" Teddy asked with a smirk.

"No, but feel free. Show me how it's done. I'll just watch." She was trying to loosen up, to live in the now, as Kiki would say. She slipped off her clogs, then put them back on.

"Gather into teams!" the emcee announced. "It's time for the Tuchus Trot! The one. The only. Well, not the only, but the best. New Year's! Nude! Relay! On your mark . . ."

There were bodies and body parts everywhere. White skin and dark skin and tan lines and no tan lines. Floppy love bananas and others at full mast. Hairy tree-trunk legs and scrawny chicken legs. Girls with no hips who looked like guys and beefy guys with boobs who looked like girls.

"This is weird," Chloe said. Weird to be with the guy she had wanted to sleep with once upon a summer, weird to be with that guy and be dealing with *This*, weird that she didn't have a clue whether he'd gone ahead and slept with someone new anyway, and weird that, despite all the weirdness, she still felt weirdly turned on.

"Pretty weird," Teddy agreed.

"Do you wonder, Where are these people's clothes?" Chloe asked.

"No! Really? That's what you're wondering?"

"Did they come here naked or, if they didn't, how will they ever find their jeans? Everybody came wearing jeans, right?" Chloe sucked her stomach in, wanting to measure up to the better half of the bodies around her.

Teddy kissed her quickly, grazing her neck. "I've missed you and your self."

Chloe decided that kiss didn't count. If she was going to allow herself just one, she wanted it to capture the wild, whirling, anything-can-happen spirit of the night.

"Get set . . . rampage!"

Hoots erupted from all directions.

And here was the thing: Every time Fig or Kiki had talked up the relay, it had seemed like a joke, a hippie-trippy joke. But Chloe didn't feel cynical now.

The night was beautiful. The air was calm, the stars were out, and the ground was soft. And she was with people, swaying people, blissful, peaced-out people, people open to possibilities. And wasn't that all you could ask of someone? To be open to possibilities? Chloe had the sense it was the kind of bright night when only good things would happen.

"Want to go somewhere where people have more clothes on?" Teddy asked.

"What about MJ?" Chloe asked.

"What about her? She's a big girl."

Not one part of Chloe wanted to say no.

Past the Japanese garden and past the tennis court, Teddy and Chloe sat on the patchy grass, leaning against a redwood tree.

Teddy walked his fingers up Chloe's leg, under the hem of her jeans skirt. A ribbon of sweat broke out behind her knees.

Oh, man. Chloe twisted and kissed him. At first, it felt like summer—hot and juicy—but then the kiss turned different. Darker, closer. With her eyes trembling closed, Chloe saw Teddy morph into Shep. She pulled away.

Teddy was just Teddy, but Chloe needed to inhale long and deep. She ran her tongue over her teeth. Had she brushed? She had. Teddy slid his hand up Chloe's back.

"I have to go," she said, but then she didn't move. She pulled a strip of bark off the tree and separated it into strands.

Teddy undid Chloe's braids. "Go later."

She really wanted to go not at all. Chloe saw Teddy's jeans all swelled up at the crotch. She looked out in the direction she thought of as ocean, but it was dark and she could have been looking the wrong way. It would be a great time for a distraction—a rogue wave or one of San Francisco's infamous tremors, which would, in some bizarre way, echo the thrash of her stomach. It was quiet.

So she kissed him again, making the kiss a whole story, giving it a beginning, a middle, and an end.

Chloe stood up and brushed off her jeans skirt, because she should and she still could. She'd given in just enough, a minor tremor that didn't open any major fault lines.

And then she willed herself to walk away, even though Teddy stayed put, and even though not a single cell of Chloe was psyched about the good-byeing.

IMPROMPTU FONDUE

Much later that night/morning, after Chloe had swallowed all her Teddy feelings, after she had found Kiki and the two of them were karate-chopping the legs of the condom table flat, Teddy reappeared, alone and slightly dazed.

Kiki swiveled her head from Chloe to Teddy and smiled. "Nice to see you again, box boy." She was still buzzing from her performance, *Under Where*. Chloe'd missed it, but Kiki said there were two encores.

"Oh, hey," Teddy said to Kiki. "I just need Clo for a second."

Kiki smiled. "Hippie New Year," she said, then disappeared in search of Fig and the keys to the wagon.

"I'm lost," he said to Chloe. "You're hot, you're cold, you're seventh grade. I can't figure you out, and it's making my head hurt. I didn't want to bail without a good-bye, even though I guess that's what you were trying to do. So bye. I'm going to take off and catch you next time."

He picked up a stray condom, still wrapped, from the grass and took a pen out of his pocket.

"Wait, hold this," he said to Chloe, handing over the pen.

"Why?" But she did.

Teddy unwrapped the condom, unrolling it and stretching it over his knee, a makeshift writing surface. "Pen?"

It was a Magic Marker, black and fat.

Teddy wrote *l-o-s-t* on the condom. He blew it up and let it whizz off, streaming air. "That, my friend, is love lost." He said it with a smile, but his eyes were serious.

"Do you mean . . ." Chloe couldn't find the words to ask if he meant he'd wanted to "make love," as Kiki would say, or if he was, literally, blowing her off. Either way, she didn't want to be lost as much as found. Either way, he was here, right here.

"Where's MJ?" Chloe blurted out.

"Getting to know my roommate."

"And you won't ever tell her about us, right? I probably sound all Girl Scouty, but promise me."

He laughed. "Sure. Aside from the yuck factor, though, I don't think she'd really care."

"You never know, though."

In that whizzy instant, and with that promise, Chloe decided she could revise her plan. She could kiss Teddy again and still be in control. She'd already kissed him once, and the world hadn't imploded.

The air inside Teddy's old Corvair was warm and apple-smelling, like it had previously carried pie.

"Let's look at the Golden Gate Bridge from down below," he said, shifting into drive. The tennis courts were still lit, waiting for action.

Teddy turned down Van Ness, then left on the busiest part of Lombard, past a string of cheapie motels with too-bright neon signs blinking VACANCY.

"Isn't it weird that Golden Gate Park isn't near the Golden Gate Bridge?" Chloe asked.

No answer from Teddy. Maybe it was a stupid question.

The bridge loomed to the right, lit so its pillars and cables looked phosphorescent orange.

"The Safeway at the marina is open late." Teddy yanked into the parking lot.

The supermarket was empty. Teddy went in search of a few bottles of Heineken, and Chloe looked for strawberries. She had a sudden craving.

At the checkout lane, Teddy kissed Chloe's thumb. His lips stayed put, warm and calm.

Chloe thought back to the day before Teddy took off for Berkeley. They'd hiked Quartz Peak, this point on the spine of Sierra Estrella, half an hour outside of Phoenix. It was one of those perfect weather days with a too-blue sky, the kind of day that makes people leave their snow tires behind and plant themselves in Arizona to begin with. Everything looked fake. Hiking to the first plateau was easy, and that was where a lot of people turned around. But Chloe and Teddy trekked to the crest, another two hours up a single-file, switchback trail. At the summit, Teddy sat, legs crossed, and Chloe sat in the open space in his lap staring out at the great divide. They'd passed a melted chocolate bar back and forth.

"Hold on," Chloe said as the cashier started to ring up the berries. To Teddy she said, "Aren't you in the mood for celebratory fondue?"

He cracked up. "Uh, am I?"

"Wait here." Chloe ran aisle to aisle, collecting one of those disposable aluminum foil pans, a candle, toothpicks, a box of matches, and two bars of Ghirardelli chocolate.

Teddy was still in line, chatting up the cashier, when Chloe got back. "We'll improvise," she told him as he picked up the foil pan quizzically.

On the lawn near the Saint Francis Yacht Club, with the Golden Gate as a backdrop, Chloe and Teddy ate strawberries and not entirely melted chocolate.

Teddy tipped back his beer and said, "You're the same, but different."

Chloe took the smallest of sips from her bottle. "I'm not really the same."

Teddy directed Chloe's chin with his pointer finger and kissed her, sweet and slow.

Everything had voltage: the view, the chocolate, the night, the kiss. Chloe felt this intenseness with Teddy—she'd felt it all last summer, as if their kisses were a kind of conjoined love. It wasn't that way with Shep. With Shep it was parallel play—his hands, her hands—but even when they did the deed, she hadn't felt intertwined.

After the tenth or twentieth or fiftieth kiss, Chloe got the sense that being with Teddy was messing with her head. But it felt good, and tonight, she thought, that line between good/bad and black/white was on the move.

Chloe gulped some fresh air.

Teddy undid her bra, and his hands slowly kneaded her back,

moving to the front. That part was amazing, but then Teddy put his hand on Chloe's stomach and she shot up.

"Back to what you said before. I'm definitely different." She squirmed her bra into place and tucked in her shirt.

"Nobody stays the same." He pulled her shirt free again and traced those damn circles on her back.

"I can't," Chloe said, lying back on the grass, still untucked.

"Really? All right, but I can't say I'm not bummed," Teddy said, lying next to her, covering her with his heavy cord jacket lined with something sheepy.

"Me too," Chloe mouthed.

They stayed that way a long time. Chloe turned to put her ear on Teddy's chest and thought she heard the lub-dub-lub-dub of his heart, but it might have been the sound of the bay.

In the midst of drifting off, Chloe felt rain.

Teddy shook her shoulder. "Get up!"

At the yacht club the sprinklers were in full swing. Long arcs of water crisscrossed the lawn. She and Teddy scooped up the fondue aftermath, the crumpled foil and the strawberry stems, and galloped to the car.

Chloe's shirt was soaked, the thin fabric clinging to her, a sudden second skin.

Before Teddy opened the door, they kissed against the Corvair, pressing so close that there was no air between them.

And Chloe had this strange and powerful feeling that she had stopped time, if only for a few hours.

THE MIRACLE OF VINYL

The morning sky was lavender when Teddy drove Chloe back to Kiki's place. He followed her upstairs so he could pee.

As soon as Chloe rabbit-keyed the door, Kiki began the questioning: "And? And? And?" She was either already up or not yet asleep.

While Teddy was in the bathroom, Chloe said, "Well, he's still a good kisser."

"I'm proud of you! Get the cigar box out of the oven. We'll toss it out the window. Let's unleash your feelings."

"We can't litter," Chloe said, even though she really meant she couldn't let those feelings out, not yet. Besides, Kiki was wearing a POLLUTION SOLUTION sweatshirt. The environmental concern seemed fitting.

"You can always throw away bad feelings, but we'll do it later if you insist. Wait, are you drunk on love or drunk on booze?" Kiki asked.

"Uh, not on liquor."

"Then it's love! Hooray for love! You know the test of love? If you can have a conversation sitting naked in front of someone, then you know it's real. So, is it real?"

"We had a conversation while surrounded by other naked people."

"Close enough."

When Teddy came out of the bathroom, Chloe went in to double-brush her teeth and to floss. In particularly stressful times, she'd been known to brush three times, then hose her gums with a Waterpik.

"Things are cool between us, right?" Teddy asked as he put his sheepy jacket on near the wooden beads.

"Perfect," Chloe said. Aren't the best lies the kind that make people feel good? Chloe thought she'd read that in *Seventeen*. That it was okay to pretend you liked someone's bangs or pretend her cords didn't make her ass look huge.

"Good." Teddy leaned in for the most gentle kiss.

Chloe thought of how naturally they fit together, girl/boy, past/present, love/lust, truth/lie, either/or.

At that moment, MJ tripped through the door, wearing a daisy-chain crown.

Chloe tried to pull away, but Teddy's hands stayed laced around her waist.

"Hey," Teddy said, "sister, sister."

"Whoa. Whoa, whoa, whooooooa." MJ shook her head, and petals flew. "What are you doing?"

"Not much." Teddy shrugged.

"Were you *kissing*?" MJ asked.

"No biggie," Teddy said.

"MJ, it was *nothing*," Chloe said.

"How is KISSING Chloe no big deal?" MJ said to Teddy. She seemed very awake.

Kiki offered up, "A good kiss is hard to find." As Virginia would say, Kiki was fanning the flames.

Teddy turned to Chloe. "I know what we said last night, but what the hell, let's tell her."

"Excellent!" Kiki chimed in. "Let it all out."

"Tell her WHAT?" MJ's eyes were huge.

Chloe shook her head. "Not now, Teddy."

"Are you taking advantage of Chloe?" MJ asked. "She is in a tough spot. Be a good guy and just let her be."

Teddy stepped on the end of MJ's line. "It's okay, MJ. This is not some one-night thing. We're good, me and Clo. We've been hanging a while. We didn't want to tell you over the summer, in case we puffed out or in case you'd think it was too . . . tangled. But I'd say we're good." He squeezed Chloe's shoulder for emphasis. "Clo, what would you say?"

"I'd guess I'd say . . . I'm sorry." Chloe made herself look at MJ.

"Wait! For a *while*, Clo? How can it have been for a *while*?"

"It was when you were away," Chloe said.

MJ held on to her peace sign. "Away?"

"You were *away*," Chloe repeated. It occurred to Chloe that MJ might think she was lying about Shep. "Teddy and I were just in the summer, not in the fall. Not in the fall *at all*."

And then MJ couldn't stop talking. "Remember our drive over the bridge? Oh, weren't we in this together? And remember later that night at the bar? I do. I've got a fabulous memory. So, *Clo* . . . let's tell Teddy why you're really here, then. He deserves to know. In the spirit of honesty, right?"

"I was thinking about that. That's my thing to tell." Chloe wrapped her arms around her shoulders, wanting to swaddle herself in some kind of protection.

"Maybe it was your thing a week ago," MJ said, her lower lip trembling. "But now you're messing with *my* brother, with *my* family, and it's *my* business. Confession cleanses the soul."

"Why are you doing this?" Chloe asked.

"ME? Ask yourself. Go on. Confess that you've got an appointment at the hospital in two days." MJ's eyes were fixed on Teddy.

"Are you sick?" Teddy asked, his eyes darting between the two girls.

Kiki climbed up on the kitchen stool to make an announcement. "Something beautiful was happening here. Let's get back to the beautiful part," she said, but then she didn't seem to know what to say next. She stood there, looking stunning and lost.

Chloe looked past Kiki, out the window to the still-lavender sky, which had been full of promise only a few minutes ago. She took a long breath that started from her grass-stained feet, evading everyone's eyes. "I'm having a thing—an abortion. Monday."

"Wait. Why?" Teddy asked. "Are you pregnant?"

"That's the way it works, Einstein," MJ said.

That stirred Kiki, still up on the stool, one arm raised like a bohemian Statue of Liberty. "Let's not be cruel here. Cruel isn't cool."

"But we didn't—" Teddy said.

MJ said, all staccato, "She. Slept. With. Shep."

Chloe surprised herself by not wanting to cry. "You think I planned this? I didn't even like it, not really."

Teddy checked out the floor. "You had sex with Shep?"

Chloe filed away that she wished Teddy had asked about her and not Shep. "You and I broke up. We broke up. And, anyway"—she straightened her shoulders and pulled herself up just enough to see the scene from a bird's-eye view—"at some point, everybody has sex, right, unless they're a priest or a freak. For years you're a person who hasn't done it and then, wow, you're on the other side. You look around and think, *That* person has had sex! *That* person has had sex! Even the guy unloading cases of Ritz crackers at the grocery store has had sex."

"So it's no big deal. You'll have it with anybody," Teddy said. "The Ritz guy—is he next?"

"No! It was one guy, and not even the right guy. And you had sex too! You told me all about senior year with Renee Rhodes. Why is it you can and I can't?"

Teddy shrugged. "You could have told me."

"How? How could I have told you?" Chloe wanted it to be later in the day, to be having this conversation after some sleep, not after a night with Teddy. "And I wasn't stupid. We used a condom."

MJ was shaking, not a lot but noticeably. To Teddy she said, "Stand here, next to me."

"But you were kind of stupid," Teddy said, staying close to Chloe. "You're pregnant. And you didn't even like him."

"Look at me, Teddy—we've got you in a box." Kiki stepped down from her stool and opened the oven to take out the cigar box. "Chloe is absolutely not stupid."

"Forget the fucking box," Chloe said. Her mouth wasn't as profane as everyone else's. When she swore, she got the floor. "I'm not the first girl in the world to get pregnant. They did abortions in ancient Greece, right, MJ? Thank you, World Civ."

"But that—" MJ interrupted.

"I'm not done," Chloe said. "What about adoption? That's what a nice nurse asked me: Am I interested in adoption? Well, guess what? I'm not. To have a kid—" Chloe drew a sharp breath in. "Well, that's putting it out there, you know? It would haunt me forever to put a person out in the world and not take care of it. An abortion so early . . . when the thing is less than a freaking inch . . ."

Chloe scanned the table near the turntable for something that was half an inch. Everything was bigger. Everything.

"Maybe I'd have a miscarriage next week anyway and I'm just pushing the inevitable, the half inch, along. That's how I'm thinking about it."

"The prosecution rests," Kiki said, a big smile plastered on her face.

A vein on MJ's forehead popped out. "Kiki, you're blind. Chloe is manipulating all of us! She just wants you along so she doesn't have to forge a note from Virginia. Like that's the *worst* thing to do . . . after she's lied to everybody."

"I was trying to protect everyone," Chloe said. Maybe she was just trying to protect herself. Maybe her inside picture of who she was didn't include a person who would forge an approval of abortion or need one in the first place.

MJ shook her head. Bits of dried daisy littered her scalp, petal dandruff.

Teddy's hands were so deep in his pockets, his jeans were sliding down.

A few tight tears slid down Chloe's nose.

The front door snapped open, and Fig strode in without a shirt. He looked skinny when he was in clothes, but half naked he was flabby, like a father. "Jeez, who died in here?"

No one answered.

"Well, I'll dream of conga drums by myself, then," he said, heading to the bedroom.

MJ walked out, Teddy at her side, their four arms pumping like a well-oiled machine ready to move onward.

Kiki sat next to Chloe on the window seat.

"We could still throw away the box of your feelings for Teddy, but for a different reason," Kiki said.

"It wouldn't change anything."

"So what?"

Chloe drew circles on an album on the floor with her big toe. "Is there an album here you hate?"

"Help yourself." Kiki took a stack of albums and dropped them in the center of the floor. "Not the Joni Mitchell, but I don't give a flying fuck—or Fig—about the rest."

Chloe palmed the Beach Boys' *Pet Sounds* from its cardboard. She remembered Teddy thought it was a minor masterpiece.

"What if I chuck this out the window?"

"*Do it,*" Kiki said. "I have a friend who works at Tower. Most of these were free. Easy come, easy go."

The window was used to being thrown open for rabbit-foot key delivery. Chloe held the record firmly, sensing its weight and size, and curled her wrist back.

Then, *flick.*

The album Frisbeed out the window. Chloe watched it drift down and land on the sidewalk.

"Keep at it. I'm going to join Figgy," Kiki said, walking backward out of the room.

Donovan, *flick.*

Dr. Byrds & Mr. Hyde, flick.

Mott the Hoople, *flick.*

Penitentiary Blues, Déjà Vu, Jesus Christ Superstar, Tea for the Tillerman, and, finally, Ry Cooder.

Flick, flick, flick, flick, flick.

Chloe leaned out the window, assessing the damage. Vinyl was pretty sturdy. The albums broke in big, jagged shards. Their cardboard centers—the music nuclei, in orange or red or white or yellow or aqua—were all intact.

She wanted to leave the mess right there, vinyl litter, as proof that she felt cracked. And she did, for a good five minutes, before she couldn't stand it.

Chloe ran downstairs barefoot, dodging dog poop and red ants, to pick up the various album pieces now damp with fog.

It would be fantastic, she thought, to jigsaw the pieces together in a whole new way and, somehow, end up with an LP that would fix *This* or erase the rest.

She couldn't, of course. So she went back up to take a nap with her tall stack of broken song pancakes.

DEAD GIRL FLOAT

Chloe had a fried brain. She'd gone over the whole night and morning, the kisses, the condoms, the strawberries, the sprinklers, but it always ended the same way, with MJ and Teddy walking out the door, and Chloe feeling raw and shocked and alone.

New Year's Day was a blur of TV, of *All in the Family*, *Funny Face*, *The New Dick Van Dyke Show*, *The Mary Tyler Moore Show*, and *Mission: Impossible*. Kiki and Fig ducked out for a morning-after party, and when they came back, Chloe was still glued to the tube.

It wasn't until the next morning that Chloe, still dressed in her unraveling denim skirt, even felt like getting off the window seat.

Fig left to return the station wagon, Kiki retreated to the tub, and Chloe flossed, using the oven door as a mirror. She had a terrible taste at the back of her throat, a curdled aftermath of yesterday combined with her usual morning sickness.

Plus, she was starving, and there was no bread. Chloe made a PB and J on a leftover sweet potato. She thought it was good practice, learning to improvise. No bread, find a vegetable. No friends, find yourself.

It had been half an hour, and Kiki was still in the tub.

Chloe washed the dishes, and in her peripheral vision she saw a coffee can on the windowsill, crammed with wooden spoons and ballpoint pens and colored pencils. She would need the note from Virginia, or make-believe Virginia, tomorrow.

But it was weird. Instead of grabbing one of the Bic pens, Chloe reached for a pair of scissors standing tall in the middle, a blade bouquet.

In the name of whatever—the Now, the Nude Relay, the Kiss, the broken albums, the *This*—Chloe had a wild urge to look different. She felt, simultaneously, better/worse, liberated/guilty, honest/deceitful—but more than anything, she felt *different*.

She held the scissors against her cheek. They smelled metallic, like coins or maybe blood.

It surprised Chloe how steady her hand was. She pressed a small section of hair between her index finger and middle finger, stretching all the curl out. When her hair was straight, which it never was, it nearly reached her waist.

The only legit mirror in Kiki's place was in the bathroom, and Kiki was still in the tub.

Tilted in front of the window, from an angle all the way to the right, Chloe could make out her outline. Looking back at her were squares of herself.

She considered the best way to approach the cut, ultimately deciding to tame the curls into two Pippi braids, the same kind of braids that MJ had called little-kiddish two nights ago . . . and that Teddy had ultimately unraveled.

With her nail, Chloe started to part her hair. And then she thought, Screw it. She wasn't after some magazine-perfect pageboy. She was after release.

Turning her back to the window, Chloe poked the blades in and out of her hair, slicing into random curls. She closed her eyes, feeling her way around her head, hearing nothing but the *zjh-zjh* of the scissors.

It took twenty minutes. By the time her hair was up by her chin, the floor was littered with corkscrew curls. A bunch of surprised little o's. Before sweeping up, Chloe blew on them, imagining the curls were feathery dandelions and she was making a wish for . . . for what? Friendship, love, family, something that didn't feel lonely.

When Kiki reemerged from the bath, pink and clean, Chloe was reading a book.

"Interesting," Kiki said, dropping her towel. "I'd say it's time we get out of the house."

Kiki suggested a swim. Chloe thought it sounded like a good idea— the epitome of peace with a chaser of chlorine. And besides, a pool was as good a place as any to ask the question that hung over the hangover of the day: Would Kiki go with Chloe tomorrow?

Over the years, Kiki had bribed the custodian at the Y with many a plate of brownies—no nuts, no weed—so that, when she knocked on the door that Sunday, he opened up the indoor pool even though it was officially closed. When Kiki had first moved to San Francisco, she lived at the Y, in the apartments overlooking Chinatown, and she and the custodian were still buds, sharing a thing for steamed dumplings, brownies, and silent pools.

Chloe knelt on the concrete deck and cupped her hand to the water. The temperature was perfect. As she lowered herself into the shallow end, the water bled over the long-sleeved Capezio leotard she'd borrowed from Kiki. After that night of nude runners and their furry parts, Chloe was happy to feel almost fully clothed in the pool. She hoped Kiki wouldn't decide it was an excellent afternoon for skinny-dipping.

Kiki climbed the high-dive ladder and took a running start. Chloe used her hand as a visor to see Kiki bounce high, grab her knees, and splash fast and hard into the deep end in a perfect cannonball. Coming up for air, Kiki readjusted her bikini top—embroidered with a sunset across one boob—and hoisted herself to the side.

It was normally Chloe's style to inch along the pool's edge, not ready to fully commit to being all wet, but she'd just chopped her hair and clearly wasn't in a tentative mood. She dunked.

"Want to do laps?" Chloe tugged the leotard over her hips.

"Nah. I'm gonna pretend we're outside. I could use a fantasy tan." Kiki pointed to her stomach. "Pale as milk." Kiki hoisted herself out of the water and lay on the indoor deck. She closed her eyes.

Up and back, back and up, Chloe found her rhythm, created her own wake. A few laps of freestyle, a lap of backstroke, a round of butterfly. When she flip-kicked on the shallow side, she submerged. For a change of scene, Chloe stopped and lay, ass-side down, on the smooth bottom of the pool. Dead girl float.

She had baby on the brain. Chloe wondered if this was what it felt like to be *This*. Floating weightless in a colossal pool—nothing but room. She was free, nothing sinking her down, except her heavy mood. From down there, looking up, the lane rope and its bouncing blue balls were indistinct, blurry, one ball after another, like a string of beads.

It gave Chloe the heebie-jeebies, and she shot up. She reached up to wring out her hair and laughed when she remembered most of it was gone. She liked that she wouldn't be able to forget this week for as long as it would take to grow her hair back, or longer.

The last time Chloe had been at one with chlorine, Teddy was by her side. It was in the break room at the school pool early last summer that Chloe first noticed MJ's brother had turned cute. He had shoulder-length hair and, even though it was dark like MJ's, it was turning lighter at the tips.

"Who eats cold beans?" she'd asked, about his lunch of refried beans.

"Don't bash if you haven't tried," he'd said.

So Chloe took a microscopic spoonful—stone-cold and freckled with saltine crackers and diced onions. Teddy said he was infatuated with onions—raw onions, scallions, shallots, sauteed onions, onion rings.

Chloe and Teddy ate lunch together the next day. The day after that, she'd hung around until four, when he finished lifeguard duty, and they'd gone for a walk to the tennis courts. A girl from French III was playing with a guy, and they were decent. Chloe'd pretended to be into the game. The longer she and Teddy sat there, on a wooden bench missing a slat, the closer their thighs came to touching. Teddy smelled like summer—Coppertone and Fritos and sweat. The night lights turned on even though the courts were now empty. When Chloe had about given up, Teddy said, "I'm dying to kiss you."

And so summer had continued with incredible kisses, and more, and no one knew except Chloe and Teddy and some flora.

The thought of Teddy, of summer love turned cold, and of MJ, her year-round, decade-long friend, made Chloe kick back under, following the narrowing light to the bottom. This time she remembered the simplest thing: to blow bubbles. She felt light and good, like herself.

This time the lane rope was a lane rope, nothing more.

From up above, Chloe heard a faint voice. As she tadpoled up, she realized it was Kiki.

"Marco?" Then louder, "Marco! MARCO?"

"Polo," Chloe said, her arms leaning against the side. The leotard trapped some water on her way up and Chloe's belly looked fully inflated, like a giant person or a pregnant one. She slapped at her stomach and, *fffffff,* the leotard deflated.

"Come play with me. Watch this." Kiki climbed back up to the high board.

Chloe got out of the pool and bandaged herself with a towel.

"Woo! Woo!" Kiki screamed, and then executed a perfect swan dive. She entered the pool with a tiny plop.

"Your turn," Kiki said, when she resurfaced with a giant smile, her hair smoothed back, goddesslike.

"I've never done it," Chloe said.

"Hang free in the air. Experience it." Kiki flutter-kicked along the edge, barely rippling the water's plane.

Chloe shook her short-haired head. Last time she'd tried, she made it halfway up the ladder before walking down backward, apologizing to all the dripping bodies in line.

"If not now, when?" Kiki asked.

"First, can I ask you a question about tomorrow?"

"After," Kiki said. "Gggggggooo! Take a fucking leap."

Chloe dropped the towel and climbed the stairs. About halfway up, she looked down at Kiki. "I'm out of time. I have to ask you before I jump."

Kiki whirled her hand in a hurry-up motion.

Chloe walked the plank and curled her toes under, hard. She looked down to see Kiki looking up. "Will you be there for me tomorrow? I need you."

"You don't need me. What you need is a note," Kiki yelled with her hands cupped.

"I can't do it. I can't pretend to be her," Chloe said, feeling wobbly.

"*You* don't have to pretend to be her," Kiki shouted. "*I* have to pretend."

"And?"

"And we'll rap on it after dinner," Kiki said, waving adios. "I'm off to meet up Fig."

"Wait for me!" Chloe took a quick breath and stepped off, stiff-legged, like a toy soldier.

She was airborne for a fraction of a second and then, boom, underwater. That was it—not hard, after all.

But by the time Chloe came up for air, waiting to hear congratulations for facing the impossible, Kiki was gone, her wet footprints evaporating on the concrete deck.

Chloe walked back to the apartment solo, trying to adopt Kiki's swagger, swinging her arms, smiling at people, even though few were out that Sunday. The fog was burning off. Block by block, down the steep hill back to North Beach, every living thing—the oleanders, the hummingbirds—seemed to come back to life, from gray and dull to bright, then brighter. It was like watching a Polaroid develop, blurry then suddenly real.

Chloe let herself into the apartment with one of Kiki's bunny-foot keys. She peeled off her skirt and Kiki's still-damp leotard and turned the hot water on full blast in the shower. She ran to the kitchen to grab a scrubbie sponge.

While the shower hit the back of her neck, Chloe re-scoured the tile, really working the lines of grout, wanting to get rid of all the dark specks. The hot water held out, and Chloe kept at it, working one side of the stall, then the other. When her fingers were raw, she stopped and did a quick shampoo, hoping the Lemon Up, with its lemon-shaped cap, would cleanse her of sadness, too, which was probably too much to pin on a single toiletry item, especially now that she had so few curls to lather. She didn't bother to rinse and repeat.

Once she was out of the shower, Chloe eyed the mirror over the sink. She stood on the toilet and leaned over to see her stomach—head on, then from the side. With a deep inhale, she watched her stomach shrink in. She looked just like herself.

By then Chloe's skin was pretty much air-dried. There was a hand mirror propped up on top of the radiator. Chloe remembered the nurse at the pediatrician's office offering her a mirror a few years ago, asking, "Do you want to get to know your vagina?"

"Not yet," Chloe had said, blushing.

Now Chloe picked up the mirror, avoiding looking at the abbreviated hair on her head, and tilted it down. Amidst all the lower hair, there wasn't much to see. She vowed that the next time a medical sort of person offered her a guided tour, she'd say yes.

Later, after Chloe watched Walter Cronkite report that peace talks were on hold in Vietnam, still and always, and after the *Wonderful World of Disney*, Kiki hadn't called. And MJ hadn't called. And Teddy hadn't called. It was just Chloe and *This* for the foreseeable future.

HOMEGROWN AVOCADO TREE

Sometime after ten that night, during *Bonanza*, Kiki busted through the door with Fig.

"I hoped you'd be here," Kiki said. "You knew the way, right?"

Even though part of Chloe wanted to say "just barely," she didn't. Kiki looked especially fragile. Ivory hair, ivory skin, ivory dress with ivory feathers. It was like she was an albino bird facing extinction.

Instead Chloe asked, "Kiki, are you yourself?"

"Let's get some dinner. Fig introduced me to the most myopic hashish. Hash, meet Kiki. Kiki, meet hash. As soon as you are out of your situation, you have got to, got to, *got* to try it. Trust me."

But Chloe wasn't sure she could. "Maybe we should just stay home. Tomorrow morning is my—"

"And cook?" Kiki asked. "Great idea. We'll whip something up. Let's do a beef stew."

"I'll help," Chloe said, not sensing much of an option. "Tell me what to do."

Kiki clattered through the cupboards, grabbing various bottles and spices. "Where's my curry powder?"

"Next to the cumin," Chloe offered.

"You alphabetized . . . oh, what the hell. Thanks. Go dig for the carrots in the fridge—bottom shelf, back, left," Kiki said.

Chloe found them on a different shelf, a little soft. "Where's the peeler?"

"A peeler?" Kiki rapped the spoon against the counter for emphasis. "Too bourgeois!"

Holding a knife just so, Chloe scraped the carrots and cut them into coins.

Fig took a long shower. The water hammered through the pipes, making the walls sound alive. She wondered if he'd notice the cleaner tiles, but then decided she didn't care.

With the carrots stacked on the cutting board, Chloe ran her fingers up and down the columns. They felt tidy and orderly, something like MJ's rosary, which Chloe had run her fingers over after the Hail Mary day. Chloe wondered if MJ had the beads with her when she left. She hoped so, for MJ's sake.

"I've got a pit in my stomach," Chloe said out of the blue.

Kiki looked up from the wok. She'd thrown in cubes of tofu, a can of Italian tomatoes, the carrots, a few glugs of wine, and chiclets of avocado. "Do this. Take the actual pit." Kiki handed Chloe the smooth avocado stone with traces of green. "Go on. Take it. I have an idea."

"I don't mean a literal pit," Chloe said.

"I *know* that. You can take me seriously, even though I'm a little high. Just a little."

Chloe pinched the pit between her thumb and index finger and walked to the sink to rinse it off.

"Now scrounge around my lighter drawer and find a couple tooth-picks."

Chloe grabbed a fistful.

"Good!" Kiki said with preschool enthusiasm. "About halfway down the pit, push three picks in until they stick out like a tripod."

"How deep?"

"No rules. Just enough to suspend the pit over a little glass of water. The top will get fresh air, and the base will be under water. We'll stick the glass on the windowsill, and in a few weeks, the stem will sprout and it will be magical, the miracle of life."

Chloe felt her cheeks flush. She dropped the pit down the drain, but it was saved by its toothpicks. Focusing on the sink, Chloe asked, "The miracle of life? Are you trying to tell me something?"

"I just wonder if you're certain, one hundred percent certain?"

Chloe remembered when Nurse Liberty asked if she was sure and she said, Yes, 200 percent sure. How could that be? If she had learned anything this week, it was that you couldn't have it both ways—with friends or boys or family or *This*. Every single thing came with a breath of doubt.

Instead of overstating to prove she was right, Chloe answered honestly. "Not really."

"I taught you well," Kiki said. "Embrace the gray. The world shimmers in shades of gray."

Freshly showered, Fig joined in, his hair braided into a single short rope, making his strong nose more prominent. He looked vaguely Viking. He cued up Joni Mitchell and sang along to "Big Yellow Taxi": *Don't it always seem to go that you don't know what you've got till it's gone.*

Kiki ladled dinner into chipped earthenware bowls. It didn't really smell like beef stew—she'd added eggplant, nutmeg, brown rice, and peanuts, but no beef. The weird thing was it tasted pretty great if you forgot what it was supposed to be.

"So," Fig asked, his fork circling the air, "are you jumpy about the abortion? I hope you don't mind that Keeks spilled the beans."

Chloe started to answer, "Not—"

"Because I was thinking," Fig interrupted, "maybe you should go bigger and bolder. Don't go back to school. It's nice to have you here. It's nice for Kiki."

Kiki smiled too wide, a prom-queen beam. She covered and uncovered her eyes like she was playing hide-and-seek with a phantom child.

"People have babies," Fig said. "They have them all the time. It could be good."

"I know people have babies," Chloe said, feeling lost in this conversation. Her mouth was dry, like she'd lost all saliva too. "This person doesn't want to have one. *I* don't want to. *I* don't even want the possibility of one."

"It didn't sound that wild when I thought about it this afternoon," Kiki explained. Chloe noticed her cheeks had not one ounce of color to them. Where had her freckles gone? "I saw this mosquito on the way home. At first I thought about squashing it because, you know, it was an inconvenience. But then . . ." Kiki covered her head with her

137

hands. "But then I remembered that Virginia never kills bugs. Who am I to crush a mosquito?"

"Mosquitoes aren't even active in the winter," Chloe said, knowing she was missing the bigger point but unable to help herself from righting a wrong. "They hibernate." Chloe cleared her bowl. She'd lost her appetite. "What happened to the shimmery shades of gray?" she asked.

Kiki's eyes crinkled as she smiled. "You're so smart. That's the answer."

"What's the question?" Fig asked.

"The question is, How can I help Chloe?" Kiki said snippily. "And the answer is found in a sparkling, nearly iridescent shade of gray."

"Gray is pretty uptight," Fig threw in. "Gray flannel suit."

Kiki turned to Chloe and said, "I struggled with it all day, but now with a full stomach and an increasingly clear head, I see it. I can be behind you and also be gray about it." Kiki wrapped her thin arms around Chloe's shoulders and stayed there. "I can support you without—entirely—supporting your decision. I'm not saying I don't support your decision, of course."

Of course? Chloe had a hard time following.

"I'm just saying it's not important whether I agree or not. I can be behind you," Kiki said. She stood up and heel-toe walked behind Chloe.

Chloe swiveled her head to see Kiki mimicking her, me-and-my-shadow style.

"Not for Virginia, not for me, or for this old fool," Kiki said, tickling Fig's long neck. "Just you."

"Thank you," Chloe said.

"I love you," Kiki said back.

They made a plan for the last step of the plan.

Kiki and Fig would go to a party, as scheduled, a post–New Year thing at a quasi commune over in Marin. They might be out all night. Still, Kiki would meet Chloe at the clinic at nine forty, twenty minutes before her appointment. Fig promised she wouldn't be late.

There was no more talk of Virginia or saving mosquitoes, and Chloe slept well completely alone, except for the space inside her that would either be empty or not tomorrow morning, depending on how you viewed gray in the world.

SMOKE HALO

Chloe ripped open the bag holding her last clean outfit, a sailor shirt and new jeans. She wanted to look clean and crisp, the opposite of hippie-dippy, for this appointment. After a stop in the bathroom for two vomits, Chloe sucked in and zipped up. She felt hermetically sealed.

Chloe heard the front door open. With a ribbon of floss dangling between her front teeth, she yelled, "Kiki, I'm glad you're here. I'm almost ready to go."

"Not Kiki," came the voice from behind.

In the bathroom mirror, on either side of her new curly bob, Chloe saw MJ. As MJ moved closer to her reflection, she grew.

"Your hair," MJ said. She twisted a piece of her own still-long hair around her finger.

"You're back?" Chloe asked. Her first thought was, *You're here to help me;* her second thought, *You're here to yell at me.*

"Just getting my stuff," MJ said.

Chloe ran her hands through her hair, still shocked to find it stopped and her hands kept going. "You remember what today is, right?"

"I know." MJ balled up her sweaters and pushed them into her suitcase. "Where's Kiki?"

"She's meeting me there."

"I'm just going to stay with Teddy until it's over." MJ slapped the clasp on her suitcase shut. "We'll leave in two days, okay? It'll be an interesting drive home."

Chloe thought back to the trip that brought them here, over the phantasmagoric Golden Gate. And how, in a week and a day, so many things had unraveled. "MJ, wait. MJ, I'm—"

"What?"

"Maryjane Donnelly, I was wrong."

"About what, Chloe Switzer? About what were you wrong?" MJ narrowed her eyes a little, like she wasn't sure she could believe anything that came out of Chloe's mouth.

Chloe paused. She didn't want to toss out a flip answer. "I was a chicken. I was a chicken about Teddy and a chicken about you wanting, or needing to pray." Chloe glanced up and caught MJ's eye. "Cluck, cluck," she added.

"Cluck, cluck," MJ echoed, sitting on the futon. "You know what pissed me off? Not you kissing my brother, though—no shit, Sherlock—that was weird for me. It's that you didn't tell me."

Chloe lifted her eyebrows.

"Yeah, I know. I may not be the easiest to tell," MJ said.

Chloe sat, too. "Sorry I hurt you." That wasn't so hard, four little words.

MJ answered with the perfect five words: "Sorry I hurt you, too."

* * *

It was a quick ride to the come-and-go entrance on the side of the hospital. This time, the area was protester-free. Inside the waiting room, in the lineup of chairs, arm to arm to arm, Chloe chose a seat near the door. Kiki wasn't there when Chloe arrived at nine forty. Kiki wasn't there at ten. Or ten ten. Or ten twenty.

"Ms. Switzer?" The receptionist behind a half wall drew out the *zzzzzzzz* in *Ms.* "The doctor can't wait much longer."

Chloe tried to make eye contact with the woman, who was wearing an orange-flowered pantsuit. She asked the question she knew the answer to. "Can I do it alone?"

"I'll check the paperwork," the woman said, walking out of view. She returned a moment later. "According to your file, the Committee has approved the procedure, but there's no Parental Notification Document. You need a parent, either in person or on paper." Almost incidentally, she added, "Sorry."

"I'm sure my—" Chloe almost said *aunt*. "I'm sure my mother will be here soon." Chloe sat back down, imagining all the research, phone calls, missteps, protesters, appointments, lies, sliding down a killer hill—she remembered part of Kearney Street being especially steep. It was all worth zilch if Kiki forgot to show.

"Peace," a deep voice said from over Chloe's shoulder.

"Fig?" Chloe asked, spinning around. He was there in front of her without Kiki. "Jesus, Fig," Chloe said. "Where's Kiki? She was supposed to meet me here"—Chloe glanced at the clock over the exit door—"forty minutes ago."

"Yeah, about that. Not going to happen." He swiped under his nose, in his mustache place.

"How much longer is she going to be? This is the day."

"Bad news, Clo," Fig said, his eyes somewhere else.

Chloe felt the anxiety rise up from her stomach in a single block. "Where is she?" Chloe asked slowly. She wanted to make sure Fig understood the question.

"The emergency room at the other hospital, Mount Sinai. I think we should head over there. To the hospital, not the mountain in Israel. Isn't it weird that a hospital is named after—"

"I'm sorry," Chloe said to the receptionist. Her nose stung from pent-up tears, but she didn't cry. Who would she have cried for, anyway? Kiki, *This*, herself? "I'm sorry, but I have . . . we have to go."

It turned out there was no Mount Sinai Hospital.

"Mount Zion?" the cab driver asked when Chloe and Fig got in the back.

"I don't know," Chloe said. "Is there a Mount Zion in Israel?"

The cab driver looked confused. "I'm from Idaho."

"Okay, Mount Zion." Chloe grabbed hold of Fig's arm. "Is she okay?"

"What does okay even mean?" he said, leaning his head against the back window. His velveteen shirt was soft against Chloe's arm.

Mr. Idaho pulled up to an imposing stone building. Chloe reached into her wallet, touching MJ's squished St. Christopher for luck, or something like luck. Before she could take out any money, Fig handed the guy five bucks.

Fig held the thick glass door open, and Chloe walked ahead.

It felt wrong to be so quiet with him. Kiki and Fig were all about the noise.

The hospital looked different from the one Chloe was just in—older, grimmer somehow. Two men in doctor coats waited by the elevator, holding Styrofoam cups of coffee.

"Where's the emergency room?" Chloe asked.

The younger doctor pointed down the hall to the left.

"Chill, babe," Fig said, drawing an invisible line along the hallway with his finger. "Kiki's just pale."

A nurse steered them down a corridor to a room with a peach curtain instead of a wall.

Chloe pulled the curtain back. A different nurse, an older one, was checking Kiki's blood pressure. Kiki was asleep, snug in the hospital blanket, her face at a standstill, her eyelashes invisible.

"Is she going to be all right?" Chloe asked, her voice full of unused tears. She stood at the foot of the bed like a child.

"Seems like it. But scoot. I've got to insert a catheter, and if she was more with it, I'm sure she'd ask for her privacy," the nurse said.

"Oh, you don't know Kiki," Fig said softly.

Chloe thought Kiki looked tiny and naive, a thirteen- or fifteen- or seventeen-year-old girl with translucent skin who'd gotten stoned for the first time, a walking—or lying-down—cliché. How she would hate to be unoriginal.

Fig walked outside the building, and Chloe followed.

"What happened, Fig?"

When he didn't answer, she added, "Do you have a cigarette?"

That did it. He stopped and turned. "You smoke?"

Chloe shrugged. "Not really, but I figured it'd get your attention."

It was barely drizzling, but Chloe didn't want to feel anything against her skin, not even vapor. She huddled under the broad awning by the main entrance.

The sky was weird—swirly and sad. Fig leaned his head in, lit up, and passed one of his hand-rolled cigarettes to Chloe. She held the cigarette in her hand, letting the ash grow and grow until it flicked itself off, a victim of gravity. Holding something, even a cancer stick, as Virginia would call it, felt oddly comforting.

She took a tiny drag and liked the way the smoke burned her throat, filling her with warmth. Chloe smashed her lips together, unleashing a little lingering smoke that had been just lying there dormant in her gums. She wanted to hold the Kiki news and the tobacco inside.

With the exhale—deeper, slower, worse—came the letdown.

"What happened?" Chloe asked. "What happened? What happened? What happened? What happened? What happened?" She could feel herself losing her shit, and she was just going to keep asking until Fig filled in the blanks.

"I'll tell you," he said finally. "We left that party this morning and went to the park."

"Okay." Chloe dropped the rest of her cigarette and ground it out with her clog.

"Kiki blacked out or something. She shouldn't do acid. She's just so small, you know. Don't blame me."

"And?" Chloe could feel a vein thumping in her neck.

"Yeah, the park was quiet." He took a big breath. "It was early for the Haight. Before eight, I think. And I looked at her. She was beautiful, just resting her hair against the grass, you know? And I was waiting,

waiting for her to open her eyes. And then some dude from the park was there. And the ambulance came. And then I rode with them. And *then* I remembered you had your appointment and that I'd promised you Kiki would make it."

"Right," Chloe said, when he seemed finished.

"Yeah, I actually need a bathroom break," Fig said, squeezing Chloe's hand. "So, you know, peace."

He took off down the block.

Chloe remembered Fig had called himself Fig the Fixer, but right now he was Fig the Fucker.

Back inside the hospital, Chloe walked right into Kiki's curtained room. She didn't say anything, either stupid or profound, but sat on the windowsill and kept Kiki company, not looking at her, but three inches above her. She was in the wrong hospital for the wrong reason, and she couldn't figure out how to be in the right place with the right person.

For a long time, Chloe watched the space over Kiki's head, craving cupcakes and zoning out to the beeps of the monitors that proved Kiki was alive.

Chloe thought about Kiki's embroidered bikini and how she had dived into that lonely pool without inhibition. She remembered back, way back, when Kiki lived around the corner, the way she would kiss Chloe on both cheeks—very European, she'd said—even if she was only staying ten minutes for a game of handball against the garage door.

Whoosh. The curtain pulled back.

Chloe had expected the nurse, but it was Fig, looking lost, holding a double scoop of ice cream.

"You're back," Chloe said.

"They were out of orange carob ripple. Think she'll like rainbow sherbet?" Fig ran his finger around the side of the cone, catching a few drips.

"I think she will." Seeing Fig trying to stop the inevitable, trying to stop ice cream from dripping downhill, was enough. She stood next to him, aligned with him.

A different nurse came in. This one had a pudding face that made her words seem soft, too. "You're very lucky," she said, looking from Chloe to Fig. "Lots of beautiful high-spirited people come to us, and many never make it out."

Chloe used her sleeve to dry her eyes. She hadn't been crying exactly, but the tears leaked out a few at a time. Until she felt them, she hadn't known how scared she was.

The cone was really dripping now, running into the sleeve of Fig's suede jacket.

"Is she your sister?" the nurse asked Chloe while adjusting Kiki's IV line.

"No."

"Not your mother, is she?" Her eyes zinged between Kiki and Chloe.

"Yes and no."

"It's always complicated, right? My guess is she's going to be out of it for a while."

"How long?" Chloe asked.

"Could be days, honey. Is there someone you can call?"

"He's here." Chloe nodded toward Fig, who was finally eating what was left of the cone.

"How about a member of the family?" the nurse asked. "Does

she have someone who is really her mother or sister? There are decisions to make about treatment and such."

Chloe went down to the lobby to get a cup of coffee, even though she hated coffee. It seemed the right thing, the adult thing, to do. She sat in a plastic swivel chair and slowly turned herself around, very hokey-pokey, thinking about what had happened today and what hadn't.

When she ran out of reasons not to, Chloe called Virginia collect.

Waiting on the line with the operator, waiting for Virginia to say yes, she accepted the charges, Chloe was fully aware of the irony of having to talk to Virginia about Kiki after hesitating to talk to Virginia about *This*.

After her initial shock, Virginia was in gear.

Virginia was thinking positive thoughts.

Virginia would be in town about midnight.

Chloe stayed in the phone booth, fidgeting with the glass door that hinged in half, and dug another dime out of her jeans, along with the doctor's card, worn thin from folding and refolding.

"Dr. Thain's office," an efficient voice answered.

"I had an appointment today. Ms. Chloe Switzer. I have a question."

"I remember. You left rather abruptly, Mzzzzzz Switzer," the flower-power receptionist said. "What can we help you with?"

"There's been a family emergency." Chloe pressed the receiver against her thigh for a second and recaught her breath.

"I'm sorry for your situation." Chloe wondered if part of the receptionist's job was to say "sorry for your situation" to teenagers who sobbed after an abortion. "Do you want to reschedule?" the receptionist asked.

"Yes, please." There was no getting around forging the stupid note now.

"We can take you on the fifth."

"Thank you." Chloe had two days to deal with Virginia, both the real and the forged version.

Chloe stayed in the phone booth, insulated. She picked up the receiver, pretending to be deep in conversation. If someone looked into the booth, she hoped she'd look normal.

Even though she wasn't actually talking to anyone, Chloe hung up. She remembered Kiki's advice. You know when you really love somebody? When you can sit naked in front of them and have a conversation. Chloe felt as naked as she'd ever been. The person she needed was MJ.

She thumbed through her composition book until she found Teddy's dorm hall phone number. The guy who answered tracked down MJ.

An hour later, MJ was there.

The third question MJ asked—after Will Kiki be okay? and Are you okay?—was whether Chloe had kept the morning appointment. When Chloe shook her head, MJ let it drop.

They sat watching game shows in the patient lounge, not saying a whole lot. *Let's Make a Deal* gave way to *The Newlywed Game*. Chloe decided that if the host used the phrase "making whoopee" one more time, she would thank MJ again, even though she couldn't think of anything different or deeper to say than *thanks*. Of course, he said it again. Three times more.

"Thanks again, MJ. This is really nice of you."

"Ah, that's how family works—you show up," MJ said, flapping her hands, dismissing the significance of her return.

"Next time, we'll do a different road trip," Chloe said.

"Next time, we'll take a different *road*," MJ said. "Let's drive to Santa Fe. Or Boulder. Isn't Boulder, like, the new Berkeley?"

And with that, things were kind of back on track, whatever that meant in a city that lurched cable cars up impossible hills.

After the cafeteria ran out of macaroni and cheese and the night nurse assured Chloe that Kiki was stable—the dope pumped out, the nutrition pumped in—MJ drove Chloe in Teddy's car back over to the come-and-go hospital where Chloe'd left the Bug.

"When do you come back for the thing?" MJ said.

"Wednesday, but I'll take a cab."

"Nah, I know where to park now. I'll take you."

"Why?"

"Why not? We're moving on," MJ said, turning her hands like train wheels in a Grateful Dead chugga-chug-chug.

"Can you follow me over to Kiki's place, then? It will be weird being there when she's not."

"It's not like she's been there much."

"Still . . ."

Chloe led and MJ followed, the Bug leading the apple-pie-smelling Corvair. They parked out front, nose to bumper.

Upstairs, Chloe flipped on every single light and lit every candle she could find. The apartment smelled like a jumble of sandalwood, jasmine, pine, vanilla, musk, and the strange gasoline smell of burnt-out matches.

"Have you and Teddy talked about me?" Chloe asked, looking into the blue of the flame, not at MJ.

"Beeeeelieve me, I won't be bringing it up." MJ laughed and poured herself some of Kiki's jug Chablis. "What about Virginia? What are you going to tell her?"

"Nothing. I just need to write that stupid note."

"You want to thumb wrestle for it?" MJ asked. "Loser writes it."

"You'll win."

"Probably."

Still, Chloe circled her thumb, right then left, trying to warm it up, wanting her *digitis primus* to come through for her with supernatural power.

MJ won the first game.

Chloe stacked two unbroken albums on the turntable: Bowie, then the Byrds.

They played two games out of three. MJ won.

They played first one to eleven. First one to twenty-one.

"Uncle, uncle," Chloe said. It was after midnight, and Virginia would pull up any minute. "What the hell, let me get a pen, and I'll do it."

"Well, lucky you," MJ said. "Somebody loves you."

It was late and Chloe felt dense for not catching on.

MJ reached into her bag and took out a folded-in-thirds letter. She waved it. "I thought you might need this. I wrote it on Teddy's type-writer. All official looking."

"If you're joking, I'll cry."

"I know."

"So?"

"I had to let some time go by, a day or two days. Or I guess it was three days."

"God, you're so . . . so . . . *nice*." Chloe squeezed her fists.

MJ stood the letter up in the center of Kiki's many bunny feet, like a beacon or a totem or something tall surrounded by many smalls. "What time should I come Wednesday?"

"Just stay. Why not just stay?"

MJ walked into the kitchen and poured another glass of jug wine. "I should call Teddy." She took the long-corded phone into the bathroom and shut the door.

Chloe opened the letter slowly like it was a great gift, which it was. The letter was typed on onionskin paper, so thin you could feel the impression the typewriter made on the back, pressing each letter into the paper, making its point.

It was simple:

> I, Virginia Switzer, give my daughter, Chloe,
> permission to receive an abortion.

And it was witnessed by one Theodore Donnelly.

The permission Chloe had been waiting for, had been unable to counterfeit, was there, in black and white, or technically, ivory. She refolded the letter and tucked it back in with the bunny feet.

Around one in the morning, after MJ conked out on the futon, Virginia arrived in a rental car from the airport. She rang the bell, and Chloe threw down a pink foot.

Virginia charged up the stairs in her squeaky leather jacket and hugged Chloe too hard.

Chloe pulled back. "Shhhh," she said. "MJ is sleeping."

"Oh, my God," Virginia said, clearing her throat and lowering herself gingerly onto the window seat Chloe thought of as home.

Chloe waited for Virginia's worried words or questions about Kiki.

"Your hair!" Virginia said. "Who did this to your beautiful hair?"

LIP-SYNCHING PRAYER

"Just get what she needs. We have to go," Virginia said from the bedroom the next morning.

Around the sink, Chloe saw traces of Kiki—ChapStick, leather barrette, musk perfume—and threw the stuff in her bag, along with a hairbrush, strands of Kiki's long hair ribboned through the bristles.

"Got it," Chloe said, stepping into the hall.

"What a way to live." Virginia made a point of long-jumping over a pile of stuff in the bedroom that included a serape, a straw hat, and a mini mountain of condoms left over from the Nude Relay.

"Don't worry, Mrs. Switzer. I'll tidy up for Kiki," MJ offered.

"It's *Virginia*, Maryjane. And that's lovely of you. At least the bathroom's already clean."

At the hospital, Fig was curled up on top of a few folded towels at the foot of Kiki's bed, like a Labrador.

"Oh, hey, I'm Fig," he said to Virginia with his one-finger salute.

"Fig?" Virginia asked.

"As in Newton," Fig said.

There was laughter from Virginia, louder than the joke called for. It was enough to stir Kiki.

With one big step, Virginia was at Kiki's side, stroking her hair, which seemed to have lost all shine. It looked worn out.

"When did you . . . ," Kiki started to say but closed her eyes.

Virginia leaned in to kiss Kiki's forehead. It occurred to Chloe that the two sisters, blond, lanky-legged, freckled, were the pair. They had the same parents, the same raw material. They had a stronger connection to each other than either had to Chloe. She was an outsider, with her father's genes diluting the power.

Virginia left the room on a mission to find ice chips, and Kiki whispered for Chloe to come close.

"I screwed you," Kiki said. "Could you get it done anyway?"

Chloe shook her short hair. "Kiki, Kiki, it's okay."

"My mistake made it worse for you." Kiki's voice was hoarse.

Fig jumped in. "Just find your own poem, Clo. I think that's what Keeks is trying to say. Find a poem that's looser. That doesn't need too many commas and periods, you know?"

"Lay off the drugs, Fig," Chloe said, but she wondered: Was she too uptight and punctuated? Was that what she'd take away from this week? To live life as a run-on sentence?

Virginia returned with an entire ice bucket, her heels clicking efficiently against the linoleum.

"I'm going to get coffee," Chloe said. No one remembered she didn't drink coffee.

"And I'm going to make arrangements," Virginia announced.

While Virginia met with the nursing staff, Chloe wandered down the hallway, ending up, somehow, in front of the small, windowless hospital chapel. It was empty, except for a young guy in a knit tie and rumply jeans.

"Hey, hey, I'm Rabbi Klein," he said. "The student chaplain."

"Oh, no, I'm just wandering," Chloe said.

"A wandering Jew? Kidding. It's cool, man. I'm here for all faiths."

"Oh, I am Jewish, I guess."

His hand shot out to shake. He was wearing one of those POW bracelets with the name of a soldier pressed into soft silver metal. Chloe thought it was sad that the soldier couldn't even appreciate that a student rabbi in San Francisco was wearing his name for everyone to see.

"Are you visiting someone?" the rabbi asked.

"My aunt, but she's leaving."

"Ah, then let's say the Shehecheyanu." And he broke into prayer.

Chloe wished she remembered Hebrew better. She hadn't been inside a temple in four years. She moved her lips, mouthing the words. When the rabbi said, "And together we say amen," Chloe repeated "amen" a little too loudly to make up for it.

"Any questions?" He put his hand loosely on hers.

"Here's something I've wondered," Chloe said. She hadn't really wondered it before, but there was something weird about hospitals and something weird about finding this guy, and suddenly Chloe was curious—more than curious, desperate to know. "I sort of remember learning that Jews believe life begins at birth."

"Jews believe that the essence, the memories of self, live on. Your aunt's body may have left her for a minute, but—"

"Sorry, this is a different question. I mean *at* birth as opposed to before." Chloe let go of his hand, which she realized she'd been cradling. "I'm asking about abortion." She surprised herself by asking in a loud voice.

His eyes popped. "Didn't see that coming. My mentor told me strange shit—sorry, stuff—comes out in crisis." He shook his head a few times fast, as if to reset his brain. "Okay, I'm with you now. Jews view potential life as important, but the mother is more important. Did you have an abortion?"

"Not yet." Chloe looked down at the boots she'd borrowed from Kiki's closet that morning. The fringe swayed a little.

"How far along? The Talmud makes a distinction. The closer to viable life, the harder an abortion is to justify."

"Four weeks. Actually, almost five." Chloe whipped her head around to make sure Virginia hadn't drifted into the chapel looking for her.

"So a month, give or take. That's good." He fingered his tie. "In the first forty days, the embryo is considered a limb of the mother. It's actually *of* the mother. 'Mere water,' the scholars say."

"What if it's six weeks? The way the doctor counts, it's closer to six weeks, but I know it's four weeks." She added, "In actuality. In factuality," trying for a jokey tone.

"Well, you'll have to draw your own conclusion there. It's not always so black and white."

"Are you making this up? How long have you been a rabbi?" Chloe asked. Maybe he was still taking classes. Maybe he'd meet his buddies later and tell them about the bummer of a morning he'd had dealing with a knocked-up chick.

"I know my shit." He nodded slowly, convincingly.

And because Chloe liked him, and liked his answer, she hoped to God he was right.

A few raindrops fell on the windshield as Virginia drove the boat of a rental car back to Kiki's place.

"It's all set for Kiki," Virginia said, flicking on the turn signal before finding the windshield wipers. "I arranged for her to check into a treatment center in the Haight. She's going to pay her way by teaching other group members modern dance. Clever, right?"

The clouds were on the move, anxious to gather together. The rain plopped bigger and then it poured, too fast to be wiped away.

"Right," Chloe said, hoping Kiki was with-it enough to appreciate the irony of getting straight on Haight.

"The Fig offered to water the plants. I can't see in this rain. Can you?" Virginia asked.

"Not really." Water was plastered against the window, blurring the view.

"I'm pulling over until the rain passes us by," Virginia announced. "Open the window."

"It's raining!"

"Open the *window* and negotiate me over to a parking lot or something."

Chloe cranked the window down an inch, then another, then finally, what the hell, she unrolled the whole thing and stuck her head into the pelting rain. "Hold up," she yelled. A car splashed by on the right, followed by a truck. When the coast was clear, Chloe straightened her arm out—the old bicycle turn signal—and told Virginia to hurry over.

At a certain point, Chloe figured she couldn't get wetter so she kept her head out. As the rain pounded, sliding down her eyes, her nose, her mouth, it felt like individual drops were coming together, coalescing into one unbroken plane of rain.

It wasn't until Virginia put on the parking brake that Chloe rolled the window up. The rain was still loud. It reminded Chloe of a drive-through car wash.

"I hope we pulled over in a nice neighborhood at least. What a deluge," Virginia said, touching Chloe's dripping hair. "The hair is quite mod. It's growing on me."

Score one for Virginia, Chloe thought.

"Well." Virginia cleared her throat. "This has been an awfully traumatic few days."

As the water cascaded, Chloe thought of the "mere water" comment the rabbi had made. She turned on the radio.

Virginia put her hand on Chloe's knee but still faced forward, like she was just going through the motions of motherhood. "I'm planning on letting the tears flow. A scare like this brings us closer to our own mortality. But we can use it. We can use it for positive growth."

Chloe wished she had an airsickness bag, like they had in the pocket of the 747 she took once, so she could upchuck the bullshit.

Virginia's eyes closed. From somewhere deep in her gut, she started to groan. "Oooooh. Ooooooooh."

Chloe turned up the radio. Janis Joplin was killing it in "Me and Bobby McGee": *Freeeedom's just another word for nothin' left to lose.*

The groans got louder. "Aaaahhh, oooooooh, ahhhhh."

"CORK IT!" Chloe yelled. She shut off the radio. The rain pounded.

Virginia twisted to look at Chloe, her eyes startled open.

Chloe banged her head back into the headrest. "Even today—even now—you're spouting someone else's words. You're missing the point."

"Am I?"

"It's not about your self-actualization. It's not about YOU or even all about Kiki. It's about me. I'm here. *Me!*" Chloe drilled her finger into her own chest, knowing she was being melodramatic. "It's me. I'm pregnant, and I was supposed to get an abortion yesterday." Chloe opened the window and stuck her hand out, trying to grab a handful of water. "And I'm sad, and I'm scared. And I'm still pregnant."

For a minute, the only sound was the drum of the water hitting the hood.

"You're pregnant?" Virginia asked.

"Mmm-hmm," Chloe said.

"Wow. Wowee. How?"

"A mistake."

"Was it your first time?"

"What does it matter?"

"It doesn't, I guess. I just mean the first time should be beautiful."

"That's a totally weird thing to say."

"Is it? I'm trying to find the right thing." Virginia fumbled with the zipper on her bag. Once she got it open, she took out a Kleenex.

"Why didn't you come to me?" Virginia said. "You know I'm not a square."

Virginia started to cry, really cry. Her shoulders shook and her sobs came out in hiccups. She blew her nose.

"I didn't go to anyone," Chloe said, feeling tear free.

"I should have been here. I would *want* to be here." The Kleenex was balled up in Virginia's hand.

The rain sputter-stopped. Now Chloe saw where they'd parked: in front of a gorgeous old Victorian, painted yellow with red trim and ivory shutters and a pine-green door. Maybe that was the reason she didn't tell Virginia. Because Virginia would look at this house and feel the need to comment on the rampant sexual repression of the Victorian age, and Chloe could look at the house and feel the sunshine.

"MJ is giving me a ride." Chloe missed her hair. She wanted to swing it over her eyes, which were filling with tears, a little after the fact.

Virginia started the car and slowly drove to Kiki's place, splashing through potholes that had become puddles, sending water spraying up the sides of the windows. With each block, Virginia's deep breaths sounded less deep.

After finding a parking spot out front, Virginia twisted toward Chloe again and this time said, "I love you. Sometimes I get a little . . . what, distracted? But I love you."

Chloe sniffled.

"And I love MJ. I do," Virginia added. "But I'm here now."

"I'll do it on my own. That was always the plan."

"If it helps, don't think of me as your mother."

"What?" Chloe asked, assuming there was more to come.

But there wasn't. Virginia opened the door, and the car filled with that earthy smell that comes after rain.

And it occurred to Chloe that only Virginia, who she knew loved her in her own Virginia way, could express that love by suggesting she was not her mother.

THE BEAUTY OF GRAY

Chloe didn't sleep well. She dreamed of Kiki and Fig, MJ and Teddy. They were all boarding a flight together, arm in arm in arm in arm. The stewardess in a tiny phosphorescent skirt said, "Catch my smile." No one did.

When she woke up on the morning of the abortion, take two, Chloe had run out of clean outfits in clear plastic bags. She pulled on her dirty Levi's and borrowed a purple sweater from MJ.

"Do you think Kiki has her own room?" MJ asked. She had the wok out, ready to make breakfast. "You want eggs?"

"I can't eat before the thing. And I hope not. I don't think she'd want to be alone," Chloe said. She plucked MJ's letter from the bunny feet and put it in her bag.

"I think that's you. You don't want to be alone," MJ said.

"I'm not alone." Chloe didn't want to be so intent on her own independence and tooth hygiene that she lost the thread of what it meant to be connected, by choice, one to another. In the same way that Virginia and Kiki had a oneness, Chloe did, too, with each of them.

So she knocked on Virginia's door . . . which was really Kiki's door . . . which, in the week Chloe had been here, was really Kiki and Fig's door.

"*Entrez-vous*," Virginia said. She was sitting up on the waterbed, trying to read as the waves rocked her to and fro.

"I'd really like you to come with me," Chloe said. No *maybe*. A simple, declarative sentence.

"Really?" Virginia asked. She ran her hands down her nightgown, the same one she'd had for years, with white birch trees climbing from knees to neck. "I've grown to respect your autonomy. You don't need to ask me. It's okay."

I'm OK—You're OK.

"I was thinking about yesterday," Chloe said. "And I *can* do it alone. I just don't want to. It's big, and I have a mother. You're the mother I have."

Virginia dressed quickly in her long corduroy skirt that swept the floor and pinned a Woman's Lib button—fist clenched inside the female symbol—over her boob, making her turtleneck droop a bit on one side.

MJ chauffeured. The three of them got in the Lady Bug, and MJ drove up Van Ness Boulevard, past the shiny Cadillac dealership. Even the sky was cooperative, an optimistic blue.

At first Chloe thought there were no protesters by the hospital, but then, after MJ dropped them off, she noticed a plump woman sitting on a cinder-block ledge in front of a Japanese garden. She waved a handmade sign. "To life," she said in a voice that wasn't lively at all.

"To life?" Virginia raised her voice. "Look at that, Chloe. We out-number her. How about to freedom!"

Chloe's cheeks flamed. This was why having Virginia along was complicated.

Linking arms, Virginia put her body between Chloe and the lone protester, and Chloe had the feeling that Virginia would not let her forget she was now a warrior in the fight for reproductive rights.

"Eyes ahead," Virginia commanded as they walked through the double glass doors.

Chloe noticed right away that it was a different receptionist, one with a thin face and a chignon. It was like a do-over. "Switzer," Chloe said. "Chloe Switzer."

The only magazine on the coffee table was *Life*. Chloe flipped to a story about the upcoming presidential election. Who would face off against Tricky Dick Nixon? the article asked. Dick had to be the most Freudian name in the world.

There were different girls in the chairs than two days ago, of course, but it was still comforting. There would be a few more tomor-row and the day after that. And the daisy chain of girls that she was now a part of . . . well, they would all be okay. Emptier, but also, in time, okay.

Virginia crossed and uncrossed her legs. From her bag she extracted a paperback novel. She flipped through a few pages, then stuffed it back in her bag and stood to pace in front of the windows. It seemed her turn to be nervous.

"Chloe Switzer?" called a nurse in a striped pinafore with a stethoscope slung over her neck.

"Present." Chloe jumped up, like she was in a third-grade classroom.

"Come on back."

"What about me?" asked Virginia. "I'd like to hold your hand," she said to Chloe. Virginia's own hand quivered at her collarbone.

It flicked through Chloe's mind that she never could have planned that Virginia would be standing here and that she'd be her best self. For a second, Chloe imagined ironing herself against Virginia, feeling her slender, papaya-soft arms, maybe not the current Virginia but the mother she remembered eating too many cupcakes with.

"I'll be fine," Chloe said. And she would. She was somebody's daughter, somebody's niece, somebody's friend, but she could deal with *This* on her own. It wasn't either/or . . . or . . . both/and. It was that beautiful shade of gray.

"It's patient's choice," the nurse said.

Chloe handed Virginia her *Life* and walked through the open door alone.

"I'm Rosheen," the nurse said, unfurling a long strip of paper for the exam table, like a giant roll of wrapping paper. "I'll be your nurse for the procedure." She handed Chloe a paper gown. Paper seemed a sad choice, as if the whole day was disposable. "Take everything off, undies too—you can't believe how many girls forget to take off their undies—then hop on." She patted the table. "A quick exam and we'll clean you up." Rosheen left the room.

Chloe stripped, neatly folding her sweater and jeans and tucking her bra and underwear in the middle of the pile, out of view. The gown tied in the back. Chloe shifted the thing around to cover as much of her ass as possible and sat on the table, ankles crossed.

Rosheen came back with a small bowl and set it down on a chair. "Scoot down to the end of the table, lie down, and let your knees fall open."

Chloe did and closed her eyes while the nurse pressed on her stomach with one hand and slid fingers up her with the other, gently probing to the right, to the left, then deeper toward Chloe's back.

"Good. Keep still and keep your eyes closed if you want. No one likes this part."

"What part?" Chloe asked, her eyes instantly open.

Rosheen's face appeared at the top of the table. From where Chloe lay, the nurse was upside down. "My apologies. I thought they told you during your consultation. We start with a pubic shave. For hygiene. I'm fast, though."

Chloe squinted her eyes shut and sang silently. For whatever reason, "Riders on the Storm" by the Doors was on her mind. And it occurred to Chloe that maybe next time she was offered a mirror for a vaginal tour, she would be deforested. For better or worse, nothing would block the view.

Rosheen was right: the shave was quick. Before Chloe even got to the third verse, she felt cool air where there was once hair.

There was a syncopated knock on the door, and Chloe quickly recrossed her legs and readjusted the gown before the door flew open. With a big smile, a gray-haired man introduced himself as Dr. Thain. Chloe thought it was like meeting a pilot before a flight.

"How do you like my playsuit?" he asked, doing a little back-and-forth step in his scrubs.

Chloe tilted her head, puppylike.

"Just trying to make you laugh a little," he said. "See you in there."

"He's the best," Rosheen said.

"Will I be knocked out?" Chloe blurted.

"A little. I'll tell them you want Valium. Who doesn't want Valium?" With her *shush-shush* nurse shoes, Rosheen walked Chloe into a large room with circular beamy lights.

As instructed, Chloe sat on the edge of a rolling table. She felt the back of her gown flap open. The air was chilly.

Rosheen positioned Chloe's feet in cold metal stirrups.

A different person, possibly a man, slipped a syringe into her vein. "Count backward from fifteen," he instructed her.

Rosheen held her hand like a sister or a friend.

"Fifteen, fourteen, thirteen, twelve . . ." The room faded out of focus, and Chloe, in her drowsiness, was pretty sure she farted. "Pardon me," she whispered.

When Chloe opened her eyes, Dr. Thain was standing over her. "You did great. Just lie down for a few more minutes."

"Is it over? Did everything look okay?" Chloe was drowsy, but she was aware that the doctor, probably somebody's father, had been looking at her down there, in there.

"Yes, you're healthy. It was early."

Chloe thought of a cancer diagnosis: We caught it early.

Rosheen appeared with a plastic cup of apple juice and two Oreos, the snack of happy kindergarteners. Chloe drooled while trying to sip the juice through a straw. There were questions somewhere just outside her brain, hovering near the lights, but she couldn't lasso them.

A clock above the door ticked off every second.

Chloe heard a familiar voice: "I love you, babe."

"Kiki?" Chloe bolted up and the paper gown tore at the shoulders. She turned to see Virginia standing at her side.

"Just let the sleep come," Virginia said.

When Chloe next opened her eyes, an hour had gone by, according to the oversized clock.

Virginia was still standing by her bed, her sunglasses hooked over a patch pocket on her cord skirt.

"Where's Rosheen?" Chloe asked.

"She'll swing by soon. In the meantime, I have your instructions." Virginia flapped a piece of lilac paper. "It's okay to get up and get dressed."

Chloe's clothes had been moved to this room, still folded. She stood up to go to the bathroom to change. A bloody sanitary pad fell to the floor. She kicked it under the table-bed, hoping Virginia hadn't noticed. She knew it was a stupid thing to fixate on anyway, but Chloe didn't feel, at that moment, like having Virginia see something that came from inside her.

There were fresh pads in the bathroom, thick as bricks, and Chloe tucked one in her underwear. She didn't investigate her shaved area.

By the time Chloe was done, Rosheen was waiting for her.

"Time to talk about birth control. I can get you a prescription for the Pill."

"No thanks."

"Would you rather not talk about this in front of your mother?"

"We have an open relationship," Virginia said.

Chloe thought, We do? One day of support equaled an open relationship? "I just don't think I'll have sex again," she said.

"Don't deny yourself the fireworks," Virginia said.

Both women laughed. Virginia playfully hit Chloe's shoulder, and Chloe felt like the odd one out, but she was too tired to say so.

ONION RINGS AND OTHER RISKS

Chloe shaded her eyes to look for MJ, who said she'd be waiting in her usual parking spot around the corner. The day had turned unspeakably gorgeous and warm, and Chloe felt happy/quiet, happy/tired, happy/hurting, happy/relieved. She had on Kiki's lovely violet coat, and suddenly the thought that she was in Kiki's skin made Chloe hot. She sloughed the coat off and dropped her package of jumbo sanitary pads.

Chloe bent down to get the pads, then stopped. There was Teddy, or someone who looked like Teddy, sitting in the spot on the cinderblock wall formerly occupied by the protester, who was now nowhere in sight.

Were the drugs making her delusional? "Are you here? Why are you here?"

He jumped off the wall. "Wow, your hair." Teddy's hands went up to his own head, like he had a sudden migraine. "It's really short." Chloe was grateful that it was a statement of fact, not open to interpretation.

"Why are you here?" Chloe wasn't sure she'd asked the first question out loud.

He smiled. "I want to be."

Chloe's hand wandered to her stomach. "I don't really want you here. Or now. I might mean now."

Virginia said, "Teddy, I didn't realize you were involved."

"Hi, Mrs. Switzer. Nice to see you."

"How did you know where to find me?" Chloe asked.

"It's *Virginia*. Call me Virginia, please, or I'll sound like someone's mother!"

"What?" Teddy asked. "Oh, right, Virginia." To Chloe he said, "I bribed MJ. She was hard to crack. She was giving me the friends-trump-all bull."

"But you're here. What did you have to give her?"

"Albums," he said.

Chloe smiled. "Good. How many?"

"My whole collection. But just for a year."

"Still," Chloe said. She thought of where she'd be in a year.

There was a long silence.

"Well, Clo. Let's get you home," Virginia said. "Will MJ be along?" she asked Teddy. "She's our ride."

"Mrs. Switz . . . Virginia," Teddy said, "I'm happy to drive you. I'll drop you first and then maybe spend a few seconds with Chloe."

"Clo, you need to take it easy," Virginia said. And then her shoulders softened. "What do you want? Do you want to be with Teddy to share this?"

"What? This—*This*—has nothing to do with Teddy."

Virginia put her hand on her cheek. "It doesn't? You mean . . . Well, good for you."

"Just stop it," Chloe said. She shifted her eyes to see if Teddy was judging her. She couldn't take being judged right now. "Let me spend a little time with Teddy."

"A little, then," Virginia said. "No more than half an hour."

Chloe nodded, a lump forming somewhere south of her throat.

Teddy rubbed her hand. "Is this okay? You want to get a coffee?"

"Remember, I hate coffee." Chloe didn't move his hand.

"A Coke, then." Teddy opened the passenger door for Chloe. He took a curl that had untucked itself and smoothed it behind her ear.

Virginia climbed in the back and didn't say anything for a change, aside from a quick thanks when Teddy pulled in front of the apartment and she climbed out.

Once Chloe was alone in the car with Teddy, everything looked blurry around the edges.

"Radio? Something mellow?" Teddy fiddled with the dial, not able to zero in on a station.

"I'm sort of in the mood for silence. It's just . . . let's just drive."

They drove randomly in circles all over the city, up and over Nob Hill, around the wide avenues of the Sunset with boxy little houses painted white, ivory, peach, rose, white, ivory, then down Forty-eighth Street toward Ocean Beach, which was banked in fog, back around through the woods of the Presidio, and finally to the figure-eight road that encircled Twin Peaks.

"I know you can't get out and climb around or anything, but it's a nice view from the car," Teddy said, shutting the engine off.

To the left was the Golden Gate . . . to the right was the Bay Bridge . . . and straight down the middle was the new pyramid building, a little more finished than it was a week ago. The city looked huge and sunny and glittery.

"You'll be too out of it to remember this, but I'm going to say it anyway," Teddy said.

Chloe blinked herself alert.

"I was scared for you. That must have sucked. Sorry, that's a really bad choice of words."

"It's okay."

"I'm nervous. Shit! I just want to say that . . . I want you to know that somebody loves you. That I love you. Uh, I sound like a jackass."

Chloe closed her eyes without really wanting to. It seemed easier to absorb what he was saying without sunlight.

"You don't have to say anything back." Teddy's voice sounded like it was coming from outside the car.

"I want to, but I can't figure out what." Chloe paused. "I can't get to it right now. But it's there. It's in there somewhere."

"Yeah," Teddy said. "Good." He slid his seat back, and Chloe saw he was wearing his beat-up hiking boots.

"Why the boots? Did you want to hike here? Are you bummed?"

"Nah, I was thinking about our hike up Quartz Peak. Before I left."

"Me too. I thought about that this week."

"Do you remember the sign at the top?"

Chloe pictured the view. "I remember the view. I remember the chocolate."

"There was a piece of plywood with the words 'No marijuana. You're too high already.'"

"I didn't want to smoke anyway." Chloe laughed.

"Yeah, you do what you want. That's what I'm trying to say here. Today was what you wanted. Okay, not *wanted*, but needed. I'm not saying it was easy," Teddy said.

Chloe found herself with watery eyes. Maybe it was the drugs. "Do you think I'm easy? I wasn't. I don't think I was. Even if I was, is that the worst thing? Isn't being hard—hardened—worse than being easy?"

"Let's get you food," Teddy said. "Are you hungry?"

"Not really. I'm not sure. Maybe a little."

They drove over to Clown Alley and Teddy got Chloe a junior avocado burger. He started to hand her onion rings and then hesitated. "Ah, shit, you like fries. Do you want me to bring the rings back?"

Chloe shook her head. "Nothing in life is irrevocable," Virginia had announced while passing canapés at a cocktail party after Chloe's father had moved on. The joke, Virginia would say, was that the things you really wanted to revoke—Vietnam, Nixon, Neil Diamond—tended to be pretty well entrenched.

"Some things can't be returned," Chloe said.

Teddy grinned. "But onion rings can."

"For the rest of my life, I will be a girl who had an abortion."

"True," Teddy said, crunching through a ring. "But you'll also be a girl who taught kids to swim and liked good music when she heard it and had, has, great hair and hated coffee and loved a guy who loved onion rings."

Chloe bit into an onion ring. She considered rummaging around her bag for her toothbrush, but then thought, What the hell. She ate the second half and then kissed Teddy, onion breath and all.

It seemed like a small moment.

It was really a big moment masquerading as a small moment.

ACKNOWLEDGMENTS

It's been a fantastical trip. Thanks . . .

to my best writer-friends, Louise Tutelian Morgenstern, Coco Myers, and Maura Rhodes, who remembered bell-bottoms and bands and helped the novel and me be better versions of our respective selves . . .

to the Concordians—Lisa Liberty Becker, Victoria Fraser, Charity Tremblay, and the newcomers Lee Hoffman and Marjan Kamali—brownies to you (of the Alice B. Toklas variety, if you so choose) . . . and to Jan Czech, Tess Faraci, Marianne Knowles, Angela Riley, Robin Veronesi, and Lucia Zimmitti for, as we've come to say, the usual genius . . .

to the women who shared their vivid stories of long-ago clinic visits . . . to staff members at Physicians for Reproductive Choice and Health and the former Planned Parenthood Golden Gate for help with the history of choice . . . and to Jane Pincus and Wendy Sanford, contributors to the original *Our Bodies, Ourselves*, who were wonderfully generous with their memories . . .

to the librarians at the San Francisco History Center archives, who brought forth scrapbooks, posters, song sheets, and more from the library's incredible Hippies Collection . . .

to Cynthia Bryant, pseudo-sister and real politico, who researched the state legislation and law, circa 1971 . . .

to Rabbi Alice Goldfinger, friend, confidante, and scholar . . . and to Rabbi Jeff Salkin, who quotes Torah via Blackberry . . .

to my parents for their high-chroma flashbacks of San Francisco in its heyday . . .

to Rosemary Stimola for her quick wit and quicker reponses, and to Kate Farrell, who embraced and championed this project from its very early stages. . . .

And deepest thanks to Ralph, my true love, and to Annie and Jane, for filling our home(s) and hearts with love and mischief and laughter.